He'd thought he'd just meet the boy and be able to remain impervious to him—at least until he'd worked out what he was going to do.

But that first glimpse had brought reality crashing down on him like a load of bricks. Shock and fear had fought with something like pride as he'd stood drinking in the unbelievable sight of the small boy who had his genes. The kid was beautiful, cute.

And so sick. His heart squeezed tight. His fingers gripped the key. Inside his head a drum began beating a steady rhythm. Jamie. *Bang.* His son. *Bang.* Jodi. *Bang.*

On and on it went.

Dear Reader

When my editor suggested that Louisa George and I write a duet with an over-arching story I had no idea where it would lead. Fortunately Louisa and I know each other well and have critiqued each other's stories often, so we knew we'd be able to work together. That's about all we knew. But many e-mails and phone calls later, and after a few nudges from our editors, here is my half of *The Infamous Maitland Brothers* duet.

Right from the start I loved Mitchell and Jodi. I so wanted to sort out their lives—interfering, that's me—and give them their happy ending. But with the drama of their very ill little boy going on it wasn't easy. I hope you enjoy reading about how these two reach out to each other for the special love they need to get them through a harrowing time.

Cheers

Sue MacKay

www.suemackay.co.nz
sue.mackay56@yahoo.com

Book 2 in **The Infamous Maitland Brothers** duet
HOW TO RESIST A HEARTBREAKER by Louisa George
is also available this month
The Infamous Maitland Brothers is also available
in eBook format from www.millsandboon.co.uk

THE GIFT
OF A CHILD

BY
SUE MacKAY

First published in Great Britain 2013
by Mills & Boon, an imprint of Harlequin (UK) Limited.
Harlequin (UK) Limited, Eton House, 18-24 Paradise Road,
Richmond, Surrey TW9 1SR

© Sue MacKay 2013

ISBN: 978 0 263 23515 9

Harlequin (UK) policy is to use papers that are natural, renewable and recyclable products and made from wood grown in sustainable forests. The logging and manufacturing process conform to the legal environmental regulations of the country of origin.

Printed and bound in Great Britain
by CPI Antony Rowe, Chippenham, Wiltshire

With a background of working in medical laboratories and a love of the romance genre, it is no surprise that **Sue MacKay** writes Mills & Boon® Medical Romance™ stories. An avid reader all her life, she wrote her first story at age eight—about a prince, of course. She lives with her own hero in the beautiful Marlborough Sounds, at the top of New Zealand's South Island, where she indulges her passions for the outdoors, the sea and cycling.

Also by Sue MacKay:

YOU, ME AND A FAMILY
CHRISTMAS WITH DR DELICIOUS
EVERY BOY'S DREAM DAD
THE DANGERS OF DATING YOUR BOSS
SURGEON IN A WEDDING DRESS
RETURN OF THE MAVERICK
PLAYBOY DOCTOR TO DOTING DAD
THEIR MARRIAGE MIRACLE

This one's for my friend, Anne Roper,
who is always so cheerful and fun to be with.
Thanks to her lovely daughter-in-law, Michelle,
for her help on YOU, ME AND A FAMILY.

And for Leslie, number one fan.

Also a big thank you
to Melanie Milburne and Fiona Lowe
for way back in the beginning.
This might be late but you've never been forgotten.

CHAPTER ONE

JODI HAWKE SWUNG the budget rental car against the kerb and hauled the handbrake on hard. Her heart was in her mouth as she peered through the grease-smeared windscreen towards the small, neat semi-attached town house she'd finally found after an hour of driving around, through and over Parnell. Auckland was not her usual playground. But that was about to change—for a time at least. No matter what the outcome of this meeting.

A chill lifted goosebumps on her skin. 'I can't do this.'

Brushing her too-long fringe out of her eyes, she turned to glare at her guilt-ridden reflection in the rear-vision mirror, and snapped, 'You have to.'

Think what's at stake. 'Jamie's life depends on you doing this. And doing it right. This day has always been hovering in the background, waiting for show time.'

Before she could overthink the situation for the trillionth time Jodi elbowed the door open and slid out onto the road. The unassuming brick town house sat back from the road, a path zeroing in on the front door with the precision of a ruled line. The lawn had been mown to within a millimetre of its life, and the gardens were bare of anything other than some white flowering ground cover.

'So Mitch's still too busy working to put time or effort into anything else.' It followed that he'd still not be taking care of any relationships either.

'Some things never change.' Which was unfortunate because, like it or not, big changes were on Mitch's horizon. She was about to tip his world upside down, inside out. For ever.

Whatever his reaction he would never be able to forget what she was about to tell him. Mitchell Maitland, the man who'd stolen her heart more than three years ago, was about to get the shock of his life. The man she'd walked away from in a moment of pure desperation when it had finally hit home that he was never, ever going to change. Not for anyone, and especially not for her.

Unfortunately she'd needed his total commitment, not just the few hours he'd given her in a week. Growing up, she'd learned that when people were busy getting ahead they didn't have time for others, not to mention handing out love and affection. Except, silly woman that she'd been, she'd thought, hoped, Mitch might've been different despite all the warning signs to the contrary. She'd believed her love for him would overcome anything.

Lately she'd learned the hard way that there was more to a relationship than love and affection. There was responsibility, honesty and integrity. Things she'd overlooked in Mitch. Because of that, Mitch wouldn't forgive her in a hurry—if at all. And now it was payback time for what she'd omitted to tell him in the weeks and years since she'd told him to go.

Stepping up the path, she ignored the butterflies flapping in her belly, and went for bravado. 'Hello, Mitchell. Remember me? I'm the one who got away still mostly intact. Left you when it became apparent you had no more time for me than it took to have a good bonk.'

At the very moment her palm pressed hard on the

doorbell she noted the open windows, the curtains moving in the light breeze, heard music inside somewhere. Not Mitchell's preferred heavy rock but a country tune.

She closed her eyes and hauled a lungful. What if he's got a wife now? Or a live-in partner? But the answers to the few questions she'd felt safe asking of a colleague from Otago Hospital, Mitch's old stomping ground, had reassured her he was still single and playing the field as hard as ever. But what if the information was incorrect? Maybe she should ask around some more before dropping her bombshell. Maybe she should go and hide from the truth—again. That would help heaps. Not.

In truth, she didn't want to hurt Mitchell—at all. *Too late. You already have. He just doesn't know it. Yet.* But if there had been another way around the problem she'd have found it.

'I need to do this,' she said under her breath. 'It's life or death. Jamie's life—or death.' Bracing her shoulders, she pressed the bell again. And gaped at the waif-like woman who tugged the door wide.

An open face with a beautiful smile, long black hair falling down her back, big brown eyes filled with friendliness. 'Hello?'

Jodi's fingers combed her own straggly tufts that looked as though she'd taken the wool clippers to them. No time or money to spend on caring for inessentials such as hair. A twist of envy wound through her as she studied this woman. She'd been fooling herself. Mitch wouldn't be alone. Good-looking, highly sexed, streetwise men like him never were. 'Hello, I'm Dr Jodi Hawke. Is Mitchell at home?'

The woman smiled easily, apparently not at all concerned with a strange female's sudden appearance on the doorstep. 'Sorry, but he's at work, even though it is

Saturday. I'd say come back later but who knows what time he'll get home. He puts in long hours, always doing extra shifts.'

I know. That was the problem. One of the problems, she corrected herself. 'He works at Auckland General Hospital, right?' Just checking she had *that* fact correct.

'Isn't he wonderful? Helping all those sick kids? He's got such a lovely way with them. When our Lilly broke her arm Mitch fixed her up as easy as, and even made her laugh while he was doing it.'

Our Lilly. Mitchell had a daughter? The guy who'd sworn off having his own kids for ever? Jodi's head spun and she groped for the wall to gain some stability as darkness crashed down over her eyes. This was turning out an even bigger nightmare than she'd believed possible.

'Hey, careful. You're going to fall in a heap.' A hand gripped her elbow firmly, propelling her over the doorstep and into a small entranceway. 'What's the matter? You look like you've seen a ghost. Or as our Lilly would say, seen a vampire. Here…' The woman pushed her onto a chair. She was surprisingly strong for such a small woman. 'Sit and put your head between your knees while I get you a glass of cold water.'

'I—I'm s-sorry,' Jodi whispered to the departing woman. 'I never faint. Must be something in the air.' Yeah, something called cowardice. 'Toughen up. You're a mother and mothers do anything for their children. Anything.'

A shadow crossed the floor in front of Jodi. Carefully lifting her head, her eyes met a sympathetic gaze.

'Here, drink this. My name's Claire, by the way.' The woman knelt beside the chair and held the glass to Jodi's lips. 'What happened? Gee, one minute you're asking about Mitch, the next you're dropping like a sack of spuds.'

'I'm not sure. Must be the heat.' Heat? In autumn? 'Or something I ate earlier.' Her voice dwindled off as she sucked in her lie. The half piece of toast at six that morning would hardly do this. Taking the glass from Claire, she sipped the refreshing water, and met the perplexed gaze of this kind woman. 'I'm sorry, truly. I'll get out of your way.' Suddenly in a hurry to leave, she stood up, and swayed on her feet. Once more Claire grabbed at her, pushed her down on the chair.

'Not so fast. You can't walk outside like this. You'll fall and hurt yourself.'

Embarrassed at her unusual situation, Jodi drained the water and forced her brain to clear away the furry edges brought on by her near faint. In an attempt to divert her mind she looked around the entryway, then, through an open door into the lounge. Something wasn't right. Too neat and tidy, impersonal. No toys or children's books. Nothing to show a child resided here. 'Your daughter doesn't live with you?'

'Of course she does.' Then understanding dawned in Claire's eyes. 'I don't live here.' She chuckled. 'I'm Mitch's cleaning lady. Not his girlfriend.' She went off into peals of laughter, crossing her arms over her stomach. 'As if. I'm married to Dave, a long-haul truckie. We're saving to buy our own house.'

Relief poured through Jodi. 'I've got it all wrong, haven't I?' Thank goodness, because she really didn't want to upset this woman who'd been so kind to her. 'I'd better get going. No point in waiting for Mitch.' Back to the motel and Jamie. Mum would be busy working on her latest financial report, hoping Jamie stayed asleep while Jodi was out. But at least she'd come up with them to help out over the first few days until Jodi knew what would happen. Totally unlike her hardworking mother to be away from her corner grocery store for even a day, let alone a whole week.

Concern clouded Claire's eyes. 'Hey, I wouldn't let you stay here without Mitch's say-so. He doesn't know you're visiting, does he?'

How had she figured that out? 'No. I, we, flew up from Dunedin today. It's a surprise.' Surprise? If what she had to tell Mitch was a surprise then she'd hate to think what a stealth bomber was.

Claire headed for the front door and waved her through. 'That's all right, then. I like the guy. He's kind and always pays me more money than I ask for, and never leaves a huge mess to clean up. I wouldn't want to muck up what I've got going here.'

Once a charmer, always a charmer. Jodi squeezed past her. 'Thank you for the water.' The path wavered before her and she concentrated on putting one foot in front of the other as she headed for the car.

'Excuse me. Jodi, wasn't it?' Claire called after her.

She paused, glanced over her shoulder. 'Yes.'

'In case you want to know, as far as I can see, Mitch hasn't got a woman in his life at the moment. When he's here he only uses the bathroom, one half of his bed and the kitchen.'

Relief made Jodi feel wobbly again but she kept focused on that footpath and finally made it back to the stuffy car. Inside she rolled down the window to let some cooler air float across her face. Phew. The fact she'd all but fainted showed how much of a pickle she'd got herself into. The prospect of facing up to Mitch had given her endless sleepless nights. And now, after getting mentally prepared, her moment of reckoning had been delayed. It was killing her.

Nothing compared to what's happening to Jamie.

She reached for the ignition. Glanced at the house. Saw Claire wave before she closed the front door. Claire, the cleaning lady. Not the wife or girlfriend. Mitch really was single.

Something akin to excitement bubbled through her, warmed her from the inside out. Mitch was single. So what? He was toast, had been since the night he'd done his usual no-show. Except that time she'd been sitting in the swanky restaurant, at the table he'd booked for her birthday, drinking the champagne he'd pre-ordered, tossing up between roast salmon on fennel or venison steak when she'd seen his brother come in with his current glamorous toss. The brother she'd previously gone out with, and who'd never let her down. But who'd also never made her skin ache with need or her hormones dance the tango at the thought of him touching her. Only Mitch had ever done that.

Max had seen her, seated his date, then crossed to say in a satisfied tone, 'So Mitchell's let you down yet again, has he?'

And that had been the moment she'd known she was done with the Maitland twins. For ever. She'd taken her bottle of champagne and what was left in it, bought another, and headed home, stopping only to get a burger and chips on the way. She'd got thoroughly drunk all by herself. And in the morning she'd called in sick—not hard to do with the hangover she'd had—and had spent the hours packing. When Mitch had raced in about midday full of apologies she'd pointed to his bags and asked for her key back. 'I won't be treated as an afterthought. Last night was the final time you do that to me. I'm worthy of

more than what you're prepared to give me.' Pride had
kept back the words 'I love you', instead replaced with,
'We're over. I'm sorry.'

And she had been very sorry, and broken-hearted, but
she'd known if she hadn't stood up for herself she'd eventually have been worn down to become a needy woman
waiting and begging for a few minutes of Mitch's attention. Like her mother had with Dad. She'd done her share
of begging her father for some attention too. Dad had
spent every day and night charming people into handing over their hard-earned savings for him to invest. He'd
missed her birthdays, too.

So Jodi Hawke didn't do needy. Not now, not ever. She
stood up for herself. Had learned the hard way at ten years
old when she'd been humiliated and harassed at school
for her father's crimes that when you needed friends onside they let you down. When he'd ended up in jail there'd
been an endless stream of kids to taunt her. Turning to
her mother for solace had been a mistake. Dealing with
her own problems and working every hour she could to
climb out of the debt-laden hole Dad had left them in,
Mum had had very little time for her too.

Withdrawing from everyone, Jodi had learned to fight
back. If anyone wanted to be her friend they'd had to
prove their worth. Two girls had stood by her, and were
still there for her, as she was for them. But not one of the
trio was needy, just sometimes requiring friendship and
a shoulder to soak with tears. Entirely different.

Driving away from the house, Jodi wondered what
Mitch would be like now. One thing was for sure, he'd
still be a hunk with a sculpted body that he worked on in
the gym. And those hands. Her tongue lapped her lips.
The hands that knew unbelievable things about a woman's body, had incredibly exciting ways of ramping up

the desire that was always waiting just under her skin whenever he was near. Then there were those mesmerising blue eyes that had reminded her of summer, even on the bleakest of days. Until the end of their relationship, that was. That had been a grey day.

'It will be winter glittering out at me today, though. Mitch is so going to hate me.'

Being dunked in an ice bucket couldn't have chilled her as much. Her skin lifted, her spine shuddered, and her fingers clenched.

'Remember how quickly he replaced you. Two weeks? Or was it three?'

That did not alleviate the chill gripping her body. At the end of the day there was no denying she'd done a bad thing. The fact they'd broken up wasn't an excuse. But everything else that had happened might have been. Would Mitch understand her actions back then? Forgive her?

She already knew the answer, and yet still pleaded, 'Please, please, Mitchell, remember one of the good moments we shared and go easy on me. I know I did wrong, but I need you onside now.'

Five hours later the digital clock in the rental car clicked over to eight-thirty.

Jodi grunted. 'He's not coming home any time soon.' She'd returned to his house to find it in darkness, the curtains not drawn. As far as she could make out, Mitchell hadn't been back in the time since her previous visit.

Still obsessed with putting in the hours at hospital. That man was driven. He never wanted to come second in anything. To anybody. Especially not to his twin brother. Their one-upmanship battles had been legendary at Otago Med School. Probably still were here at Auckland General.

She shivered. The temperature had dropped when the sun had gone down. And her memories of long, lonely nights waiting until Mitch had deigned to come home and see her sprang out of the dark place she'd forced them into a long time ago. Not so surprising when she sat outside his house, in his city, the closest she'd been to him in three years.

'Back to the motel, and Jamie.' Her darling boy would be tucked up in bed, hopefully sleeping easily. Earlier she'd kissed him goodnight after a meal of chicken bites and chips, a treat that remarkably Mum had forked out for. Breathing in his little-boy smell, stroking his head, tickling his tummy, a huge lump had blocked her throat. Rapid blinking had kept the tears at bay. Just. Even now they hovered, ready to spill down her cheeks in a moment's weakness. *Toughen up. There's no room for weakness.*

What if Mitchell didn't agree to her request? There was no 'what if'. He had to agree. He might be a self-focused man but he also knew the right thing to do. So Jamie should be safe.

She couldn't, wouldn't, imagine life without Jamie in it. He was so sweet, wickedly cute, and totally uncomplaining even when the pain struck. He didn't know what it was like to be full of energy, to be able to run around the lawn shouting at the world, or to ride a bike, or to go a whole day without having to take at least two naps. And yet he still had an impish grin that twisted her heart and made her hug him tight, trying to ward off the inevitable.

A tired smile lifted one corner of her mouth. Even now her mother would be hooked into the internet, reading the stocks and shares figures from the other side of the world, impervious to anything else. Another workaholic who hadn't learned to stop or even just slow down and, as the saying had it, smell the roses.

She took a right turn to head back to the grotty, dank motel room. Back to another night tossing and turning as she argued and pleaded with Mitch inside her head, as she argued with herself. Back to check up on her darling little boy, her horrendously ill little boy, who'd been dealt a black card in the stakes of life.

A car zoomed past in the opposite direction, headlights on full, and temporarily blinded her. Her foot lifted off the accelerator as she twisted the steering wheel sideways. 'Idiot,' she yelled at the unseen driver whizzing past, narrowly missing her rental vehicle.

'Delinquent. Look where you're going.' She vented some of her pent-up anger and fear. 'You could've killed me.'

Then who would talk to Mitchell about Jamie? Maybe leaving this until tomorrow wasn't such a great idea. Who knew what might happen in the intervening hours? She hadn't tried to find him anywhere else but at home. Which was fairly silly. The Mitch she'd known would always be at the hospital. Which meant he'd be very busy. Saturday night in ED was never a picnic. She had to wait until the morning.

'No.' Her fist crunched down on her thigh. 'No. I'm done with waiting. Done with planning the arguments for and against my case. Done, done, done.' Her palm slapped the steering wheel. She had to see Mitch. Now. The time had come. No more avoidance. No more lying to herself, saying she'd done the right thing. Because being right or wrong wasn't going to change a thing. It wasn't going to alter the fact she should've told Mitch about Jamie a long time ago.

The hurt she'd known of waiting up for Dad to come

home and read her a story, or to say she was his princess, had been behind her decision in not telling Mitch about Jamie. Yes, Mitch, love him or not, would act the same as her father had. He'd never be there for his child because there'd always be one more patient to help, one more urgent case to deal wtih before hanging up his white coat and heading home.

If Mitch kicked her butt hard and fast when she told him why she was here, and why she hadn't come knocking three years ago, so be it. If he sent her packing, refusing to believe her—which was her expectation—she'd deal with that too. She'd argue till she was all out of breath. If he refused categorically to meet Jamie, to help him…then she'd tie him up and pour boiling oil over his beautiful body.

Doing a U–turn, she headed into the city centre and Auckland General, the hospital with New Zealand's best renal specialists and the most modern equipment available for what ailed Jamie. The hospital where Mitch was head of the emergency department. Where he looked out for patients, including other people's little boys and girls. Would he look out for her boy? Of course he would. He wasn't an ogre.

Over the coming days she would ask him to consider doing something he'd never, ever have contemplated. Who would, unless faced with it?

She was also about to grovel before the man she'd once loved, the man she'd never shown a moment of weakness to in the months they'd lived together.

She was about to give away her soul.

It was far too easy to find a parking space outside the ED. But despite the pounding in her chest Jodi didn't linger anymore. The time had come. Having once worked

briefly in the ED, she knew the ropes and within moments she was inside the emergency department asking
for Dr Maitland.

'I think he took a break.' A young nurse answered her
enquiries. 'Though he was talking about going to a party
tonight so you might be out of luck.'

She'd been out of luck for years. Just not tonight,
please. 'Where's the staff kitchen?' she asked the next
person. 'I'm looking for Mitch Maitland.'

'Mitch headed towards his office,' a harried junior
doctor told her as he raced past.

'Which is where?' Jodi asked the disappearing back
of the doctor.

'Down the corridor, turn right, left, left, and then try
the third door on your right,' another nurse told her.

Okey-dokey. Showtime. Jodi's footsteps slowed as she
took the last left. They stopped entirely outside the third
door on the right. Her knuckles rapped on the door. No
reply. Her hand shook as her fingers gripped the door-
knob. Shoving the door wide, she stepped into hell.

'Hello, Mitchell. Long time no see.'

The reply was a snore.

She felt like a balloon that'd just been pricked. 'Oh,
great. Wonderful to see you, too.' All her over-tightened
muscles cramped further. Her tongue licked her dry lips.
And once again her legs threatened to drop her in a heap
on the floor.

Another snore.

Jodi closed the door quietly, leaned back against it,
desperate for support. Her breasts rose on a slow intake
of air, and she studied the view. Definitely still hunky.
Those hands she remembered so well were hidden behind his head as he sprawled in his chair with his feet
crossed neatly at the ankles on his desk. But those mus-

cular thighs under the fabric of his trousers cranked up some hot memories. Dragging her gaze upwards, she studied his face.

His head was tipped back slightly, the sparkling blue eyes invisible behind closed eyelids. But his long black eyelashes lay softly on his upper cheeks, twisting her heart. Oh so sexy stubble darkened his chin, his jaw.

The air whooshed out of her lungs.

How had she ever found the strength to leave him?

Worse, where was the strength to break his world into a million little pieces?

Think of Jamie. That was the only thing she could do. Anything else and she'd fall apart at the seams.

Clearing her throat she pitched her voice higher. 'Mitch. Wake up.'

CHAPTER TWO

MITCH KNEW HE was hallucinating. Too many strong coffees. Had to be. Nothing else would explain why he thought he saw Jodi Hawke standing here in his office. He shut his eyes tight, concentrated on removing that unnerving image from his brain. Slowly raised his eyelids. There. Leaning against his door. Jodi Hawke. No, not leaning. More like melting into the door, becoming a part of it. As in an attempt to remain upright.

A Jodi lookalike, then. The Jodi he'd known had had more confidence than a one-hundred-metre sprinter. Through narrowed eyes, he studied this apparition. Worn jeans hung loosely off her hips. A shapeless, faded cotton jersey bagged from her breasts and over her tummy, while scuffed trainers on her feet completed the strange picture.

The Jodi he remembered had been a fashionista. She'd certainly never gone for the ragdoll effect. And she'd definitely never been quiet, let alone silent.

God, what had been in those coffees? Definitely something weird and potent. His eyes drooped shut as the need to continue sleeping washed over him. It had been a big day made huge after a multi-car pile-up on the motorway. He'd attended to five seriously injured people, not to mention the usual number of patients continuously filing through the department. No wonder he was exhausted and seeing things. Then a nag set up in his skull. Wasn't he supposed to be going somewhere?

'Mitchell,' squeaked the lookalike.

Jodi never squeaked. Through sheer willpower he did not move, not even an eyelid. Until his mouth let him down, demanding, 'Tell me this is a joke.' A very sick joke. But there'd be no reply. He *was* hallucinating.

'Mitch, damn you. Look at me.'

He snapped forward so fast his neck clicked and his eyes opened into a wide stare. His feet hit the floor with a thump. 'You're real.' He knew *that* voice, had heard it against his chest in the heat of passion, had felt it lash him in anger.

'What else would I be?' Her eyes bored into him, unrelenting in their determination to get his attention.

She certainly had that in spades. What was she doing here? Should he be worried? Nah, couldn't see any reason for that. But after three years she just waltzes in through his door and tells him what to do? No way, sunshine. 'A bad dream.'

She winced, and a whole ton of emotions blinked out at him from those unnerving eyes. Anger, hurt, shock, caution. But the overriding one appeared to be fear. Jodi was afraid of him? That had him standing upright faster than a bullet train. Nothing was making any sense. They hadn't seen or spoken to each other for so long there was nothing between them now; not good or bad. Yet now she looked as though she wanted to be anywhere but here with him. Odd since she had been the one to walk in unannounced.

Even in the deep quiet of night, when nothing stirred except his memory, he'd never believed Jodi would want him back. *Jumping the gun a bit, aren't you? She's probably passing through and decided to look you up for old times' sake. As if.* It had hurt beyond comprehension when she'd kicked him out and before he'd left Dunedin he'd often started towards her place to beg for a second chance, only to back off, knowing Jodi would give him most things but never that.

So why was she here? She didn't do casual. Whatever had brought her through his door must be serious.

Apprehension crawled up his back. Somehow he managed to drawl with feigned nonchalance, 'Jodi, long time no see.' Three years five months, to be nearly exact. Tension overlaid tension in his weary body. And he'd thought he'd forgotten all about her. Forgotten making love with her in the long grass above the beach in summer. Forgotten how her laugh always made him feel he could slay dragons. But he'd been kidding himself. Big time.

Now his gaze was back to cruising, checking out that wacky, totally unstylish hair, the eyes that weren't bordered with a pail of war paint, the non-lipsticked lips bruised where she must've nibbled for hours. So she still did that.

What had happened to this woman? He struggled to recognise her for who she'd been. A bright, sparkly woman with a figure any model would die for and the accessories to match. An intern adored by patients and staff alike. The only woman he'd even considered doing something way out with—as in settling down and buying the picket fence with. Everything he remembered about her had disappeared. All gone. Replaced by a stranger. Or so it seemed.

'What brings you to Auckland? I presume you're still living down south.'

'Yes, I am.' She still leaned against the door. 'At least, I did until today.'

'You're on the move? Anywhere exciting?' *What the hell's this got to do with me?*

'I don't know about exciting. But I'm shifting to Auckland for a while.' She choked over that last word. Tears glittered on her eyelashes.

Oh, God, she hadn't taken a job in ED? Here? In his department? No, don't be daft. Who would've sanctioned that if not him? Think about it. She wasn't trained to work in an emergency department. The tension in his belly backed off a notch. So, what was her visit about? Had she really turned up for a chat about old times? Nah, not at this hour of the night.

He stamped on the flare of sympathy that drawn face caused, and parked his backside back on his chair. Stretching his legs under the desk, he started at the beginning. 'You arrived today and already you're knocking on my door? Do you need a job? Because I'm sorry to disappoint you but I'm overstaffed as it is.'

'No, I don't need a job.' She swallowed. 'Actually, I will do at some point but that's not why I'm here.'

There was a relief. But the tension gripping his muscles didn't relax at all. 'So this is a social call?'

Another swallow. Then her tongue moistened her lips. And that fear in her eyes grew. 'No,' she croaked.

Mitch studied her carefully as a sense of falling over the edge of a cliff began expanding deep inside him. Jodi hadn't spoken more than two sentences to him—and, yes, he remembered what they'd been, word for word—from the day she'd put his packed bags on the front doorstep of the flat they'd shared and said goodbye. Even his explanations about helping seriously injured people hadn't softened her stance. Neither had telling her he needed just another year of putting in long hours and then he'd be set for life, would have the career he wanted and a whole lot more time for her. In the end he'd swallowed the hurt, sucked up his pride, and got on with his life. Like he did with most things. Except his brother.

But Jodi's departure from his life had hurt far more than he could've ever imagined. What had started out as fun had turned into something deeper but, being him, he'd realised that far too late. After he'd lost her. So really she'd done him a favour, saved him from himself. It had been his only foray into something resembling a proper relationship and he'd sucked at it. As he'd known he would. But he'd have liked the opportunity to rectify his mistakes.

But Jodi Hawke didn't do second chances.

Besides, he knew all about the fickleness of relationships. All relationships, not just the boyfriend/girlfriend ones. Hell, Jodi was just one in a line of people who'd hurt him by disappearing out of his life. Which was why he did the moving on, usually quite quickly. Easier to protect himself that way. But he'd been in love with Jodi—as close to being in love as he'd ever been before or since— and had hung around too long, thinking it might work out. That she might be the one to see past his disillusionment. Of course he hadn't done anything to try to keep her.

The break-up had been behind his speedy move up to Auckland. He couldn't stand the thought of bumping into her at any corner within the hospital, in any bar or nightclub in town. Shifting cities had turned into a wise career move that had helped him clear his horrendous student loan and buy himself a modest house. And he'd shown his brother he was also capable of having an outstanding career.

Damn it. Jodi did this to him in a matter of minutes. Brought back the heartache, the guilt and doubts.

Someone knocked on the door and Jodi shot across

the room looking completely flustered. Mitch shook his head at her. What the hell was wrong? This timidity was so not Jodi. Something terrible must've happened to her in the intervening years. His heart rolled. He might be wary about seeing her again, but if anyone had hurt her they'd better watch out, be prepared to answer to him.

'Hey, Mitch—oh, sorry, I didn't realise you had company. I'll catch you some other time.' Aaron might be talking to him but his eyes were fixed on Jodi.

Mitch shook his head again, and focused on the guy who ran the night shift in ED. 'Is everything all right in the department?' Hopefully it was ripping busy and he could get out of here, go to work and forget his unwanted visitor. Problem or no problem.

Aaron waved a hand through the air. 'All good, no worries. I was going to read over the terms of the TV company's visit next week, nothing important.'

How was that for an understatement? None of his staff, including Aaron, were happy about the documentary a national television company was making about life in a busy emergency department, and it fell to him to make it work, even when he agreed with his staff. Visitors in the unit, especially ones the board forced on them, were a pain in the butt, getting in the way, asking crazy questions, upsetting staff and patients. 'I'll catch up with you tomorrow sometime.'

'Sure.' Aaron took one more appraising look at Jodi before glancing at his watch. 'You should've clocked off hours ago, Mitch. We don't need you hanging around taking up space.'

Mitch grimaced. Thanks, pal. Go ahead and make Jodi welcome while you're at it, why don't you? 'I've got other things to attend to first.'

Aaron raised his eyebrows. 'Yeah, sure. Weren't you going to Samantha's party?'

The party. That's what had been niggling at his half-baked brain about the time he'd seen Jodi slumped against his door. 'I'll be on my way in a moment.'

'You won't have missed much. Sam's parties don't usually crank up until near midnight.' Aaron glanced at Jodi, back to him, fixing him with a not-your-usual-type look before slipping out of the office and closing the door noisily.

Closing Jodi in with Mitch. Again. He sucked air, steadied that shaky feeling in his stomach and tried for normal. 'Want to tell me why you're here? Because, as you heard, I am busy. I'm meant to be somewhere else.'

She didn't even say, 'When aren't you?' Which he admitted she had every right to do, that having been the crux of their break-up way back then. Instead, she surprised him. 'Mitch, can we go somewhere to talk?' Her gaze clashed with his and she didn't back off. Something resembling the strength he'd always associated with her slipped into her gaze, pushing that fear sideways. 'Somewhere quiet where no one will interrupt us.'

There was a warning in her voice that gave him the impression that something terrible was coming. Yet for the life of him he couldn't imagine what. Whatever it was obviously wouldn't wait. Which made him want to stall her for as long as possible. He didn't want to hear her out. Opening his mouth to say no, he said, 'Just give me a minute while I grab some coffees and tell the night staff to leave us alone. We'll be undisturbed in here. I see no need to leave the hospital.' Except those gathering clouds in her eyes.

'I think you'd prefer to hear what I have to say somewhere else, neutral territory if you like.' Her bottom lip trembled. 'With no one you know likely to burst in on us.'

'As you heard, I'm going out tonight.' He nodded at his overnight bag against the far wall. 'I need to shower and change so I'd prefer to get this over right here. Whatever this is.' Why did he feel such a heel? Could it be the pain darkening those toffee-coloured orbs? Did he have some lingering feelings for her? No, definitely not. Crazy idea. But he should cut her some slack, at least until he'd heard her out. They'd lived together for six months so he owed her that much. 'So, do you want coffee?'

'No, thanks. Nothing.' She dropped onto the spare chair. The fingers she interlaced were white. She looked so tiny, all shrunk in on herself, and when she lifted her head to face him he gasped.

'Jodi?' Her eyes stood out like snooker balls against her colourless cheeks. Was she ill? Please, not that. Anything but that. His heart lurched and he had to fight the urge to wrap her up in his arms. Shelter her from whatever was troubling her so much. 'What's wrong?'

She swallowed, opened her mouth, and whispered, 'We have a son. You have a son.'

Wrong, wrong, wrong. That was not how she had meant to inform him. What had happened to easing into telling him about Jamie? She'd been going to explain the situation carefully, one thing at a time, not hit him over the head with a baseball bat. Now he'd never hear her through. The arguments were already building in his eyes.

Nausea roiled up and she gripped the sides of the chair, forcing her stomach to behave. Her teeth bit down hard on her lip, creating pain to focus on. There was nothing she could do to take the words back. There would be no starting again. No second chance. So get on with it, tell him the rest.

He was staring at her as though she'd gone crazy, his head moving from side to side in denial. 'I don't think so.'

'It's true.' Again nausea threatened, stronger this time. She had to get this over, tell him everything. But he was already saying something.

'Jodi, Jodi. I don't know what's behind this but your outrageous idea won't get you anywhere.' When she opened her mouth to reply he talked right over her. 'It's been done before.'

'What?'

'You're not the first woman to try using her child to get me to set her up in a lifestyle she thought was her right.'

'What?'

'Last year a nurse from the surgical ward insisted I was the father of her unborn child. Wanted to get married in a hurry before everyone noticed. What she really wanted was the wedding, my wage packet and the supposed fancy house. She played me for a fool. She lied, she lost.'

Where was the rubbish bin? Every office had one somewhere. Her hand over her mouth, Jodi frantically looked around as her stomach threatened to evict the few chicken nuggets she'd eaten earlier.

'Hey, Jodi? Oh, hell. Here.' A plastic receptacle appeared under her nose. A hand pressed between her shoulder blades, forcing her over the bin.

Don't be sick. Don't. Swallowing the bile in her mouth, she slowly counted to ten, fighting her stomach. Sweat broke out on her forehead. Her hands were clammy. Breathe. In, out. In, out. The nausea began to recede. But she daren't pull back from that bin just yet. 'I'm sorry.'

Why was she apologising? And for what? Feeling ill? Because another woman had done the dirty on him? For giving him the news no man liked to hear? She'd hardly started. He hadn't heard the worst yet. He still didn't know about Jamie's illness. That's when he'd take her seriously. And really hate her. Because he'd understand what she wanted from him.

She lost the argument with her stomach.

CHAPTER THREE

MITCHELL PUT THE rubbish bin in the far corner and covered it with the hand towel hanging beside the basin. Who knew when Jodi might need it again? She looked terrible, pale and shaky, the fingers she gripped some tissues with trembling non-stop. Half the water in the glass he handed her splashed over her jeans.

Returning to his desk, he parked his butt on the edge and folded his arms across his chest. He studied her carefully as she sipped and rinsed her mouth. Looked hard for the Jodi he used to know. Impossible to find behind the unhappiness in those eyes. Not easy to see in her bedraggled appearance. Hadn't she been looking after herself? If he'd thought she'd been white before, he'd been totally wrong.

A tiny knot of fear formed in his gut. What if she was telling him the truth? Jodi never dodged bullets; always told it like she saw it. So wouldn't she have told him about a baby right from the get-go? Wouldn't she? Maybe not. She'd always been fiercely independent.

Not to mention the memory now flashing across his brain of how she'd called him the most unreliable man on the planet when it came to devoting time to her or anyone not involved in his work. Had even gone so far as to call him selfish. So she'd expect the same of him when it came to their child. At the time, her frank appraisal had stung. Honest to the point of being brutal. That was Jodi. And right now he'd swear that same honesty was blinking out at him.

He tried to dampen the sarcasm. He really did. 'You turn up here after all this time to tell me I'm a father. Do you honestly think I'm about to believe you without knowing more? Come on, I might not be top of your favourite people list but you also know I'm not stupid. If you were pregnant, why did you kick me out? I'd have been the gravy train.'

He stood up and headed for the door. He couldn't do this. He didn't want to do it.

You're running away, big boy.

Yeah, well, it hurt to think she'd even consider him fool enough to believe her. Hadn't she got it? Way back? Got that he didn't do commitment or that for ever stuff?

Wake up. That's probably why she never told you she was pregnant. 'What took you so long to tell me?' He ground the words out.

'I tried to tell you.'

'How come I missed that?'

Her finger picked at her jeans. 'I phoned the flat you moved to a few times but you were never there, night or day. I didn't want to spring it on you in front of your colleagues in the ED. But finally I gave up thinking like that and tracked you down at work.'

The hairs rose on the back of his neck. He knew what was coming. Hell, damn, double damn. Once again he'd blown it—big time.

'You were well and truly absorbed in a nurse. That was some steamy kiss going on in the sluice room. Her arms must've taken a month to unwind from around you.' Anger and hurt blended to turn her voice sad and low.

'You'd got over me so fast I wondered if you'd even re-membered my name.'

Embarrassment made him squirm. 'It was deliberate. To make you think I didn't care. I saw you come into the department.' He sounded like a fifteen-year-old. Actually, that was insulting all teens.

Jodi gaped at him. 'You did what?'

'Yes, well, it kind of upset me when you kicked me out but I had no intention of showing you that.' If only he'd known why Jodi had come looking for him that day. Would it have made any difference? He'd like to think he'd have stepped up to the mark.

She was shaking her head at him. 'Do you know what that stupid act did? The anguish it caused?' She sput-tered to a stop, twisted her fingers around each other and stared at her feet.

'For what it's worth, I'm sorry. But be fair, I had no idea why you were there. You still could've insisted on talking to me.'

'I went away to think it all through. That took a lot longer than I'd expected.' Did she mutter 'Months lon-ger' under her breath?

He felt beyond terrible. Despite everything he'd heard, that knot of fear hadn't evaporated at all. But what hap-pened now? What did he say? Do?

Jodi's voice wobbled but her words were loud and clear. 'Trust me, I wouldn't be telling you now if I could avoid it.'

Stopping in mid-stride, he spun back to her. 'Hey, I certainly didn't ask for this. I'm not the one making you spill the beans.' *But I am the one behaving badly. Hear her out before showing her the door. It might be quicker and easier that way.* And if there was something he could do for her then he'd do it just to show there were no hard feelings. *Sure you're not remembering how much you liked Jodi before she sent you packing? Sure you don't want to make amends just a little bit for treating her so offhandedly back then? For kissing that dazzling blonde whose name you can't recall?*

I was looking out for myself.

Excuses, excuses.

Jodi pulled herself upright and still looked small. But fighting hard. Like she wasn't about to give up on this in a hurry. A mother protecting her child?

That twist of fear grew bigger.

'Mitchell, we can go the DNA route if you want proof Jamie is yours. But I think I can persuade you with this.'

His gaze was glued to her as she slid her hand inside the back pocket of her jeans. As she began withdrawing a cellphone, a sudden landslide of emotion engulfed him. He knew without seeing whatever she was about to show him that finally everything he'd ever done, all the deliberate plans to remain unattached to anyone for ever had just come completely undone.

He did know Jodi. Knew she'd never pull a stunt like this on anyone. Knew how she would not have hesitated to bring a child up on her own. Knew that she'd love that child more than life itself. All the arguing in his head couldn't change that.

Her hand shook violently as she held the opened phone out, a photo shining at him. 'This is Jamie. Your boy.'

He stared and stared at that phone, unable to reach for it because the moment he did he was finished. Life had come full circle on him. He'd spent years perfecting avoidance of commitment. Even his town house was just a building to sleep and shower in. His mouth was drier than a summer wind. His insides tossed and turned as though in a tumble dryer.

'Mitch, take it. Please.' A tear oozed from the corner of her eye.

He had always been able to turn a blind eye to women's tears. Until now. That solitary drop of water inching down her cheek arrowed straight to his heart. Jodi. Jamie.

His fingers weren't steady, probably never would be again. The phone slipped through her hand and his to the carpeted floor. Jodi didn't move to pick it up, sat there peering up at him with those stricken eyes. Finally he reached down, swooped it up, turned it the right way round and, with a suck of air, met his son.

He stared at his own reflection. At least, that's what it looked like. The eyes looking out at him were the same shade of blue he saw in the mirror every time he shaved. The only difference about the straight dark hair was the style. Slightly too long and wild. The generous grin with even, white teeth; the straight, pointed nose. Even the 'to hell with the world' attitude in the little lad's stance. This was himself thirty-three years ago.

But this photo. The modern background and clothes. This *was* different. Not even he could deny this boy was his.

Jamie was his son. He was a dad. *Oh, my God.*

'Mitchell?' His name hiccupped off Jodi's lips.

'Why now? Why not three years ago?' He swallowed the bitter comments hovering on his tongue. He mightn't want to be a father, or to even know he was one, but she should've told him, given him the choice of what to do about the situation. Except Jodi knew him all too well, had known he'd resist with every fibre in his body. What had changed her mind about telling him?

Jodi grimaced, went back to twisting her fingers round and round. The desolation in her face drilled him. 'I am very, very sorry.'

He waited quietly, while his heart thudded hard against his ribs. He couldn't have enunciated a word if he'd tried. *I've missed out on so much. Three years of growing up that I'll never know about.* Surprising how much that hurt. Even when it was partially his own fault. Especially because of that. Jodi had carried the weight of his blind need to protect himself, had paid the consequences. Until tonight. 'Tell me what brings you here now.'

When she finally answered it was with dignity. 'Jamie's very ill. He's going to die if I don't get the right care very soon. You might be able to help him.'

The strength went out of his knees. Gripping the edge of the table, he held himself upright. He'd asked and got the answers. Damn it. He stared at her. Her unwavering gaze spoke the truth. All of this nightmare was true. All of it. And more. His head whirled with angry questions. With denial. With acceptance. With—he didn't know the hell what with but it sure as blazes hurt. Pain needled him, squeezed him, shook him like a defenceless kitten in a dog's mouth.

Groping for his chair, he sank down into it and dropped his head into his hands. Could he rewind the clock an hour? Back to when the biggest problem he'd had was keeping his staff happy during the coming week? Back to when he'd been snoozing before going to a party?

'What do you want from me?' He didn't recognise his own voice it was so croaky. 'Money?' He lashed out, trying to step through this mire of problems he'd never expected to have, trying to come out on top of it all. His way. The way he felt safe. The way he had some control over everything.

'I'll forget you said that.' Ice chipped off Jodi's words. 'Jamie has renal failure. Cystinosis, to be exact. Our specialist in Dunedin believes he's got a better chance up here. In this hospital.'

'Bloody hell.' Mitch leapt up and strode across the room, turned at the wall, strode back. Turned and slapped his hands on his hips as he bent down towards her. 'Kick me in the guts, why don't you?'

'I know how you must be feeling.'

His eyebrows disappeared over the back of his head and his jaw clanged down on his chest. The situation got the better of him. 'You know how I'm feeling? That's rich.'

Her eyes were murky, like mud. Wet, brown and so, so sad. 'I've been dealing with Jamie's illness all his life. But I haven't forgotten the day I was told about his condition. The terror, the sense of failing my baby, wanting to believe the doctors had made a mistake and that someone's else's son was sick and not mine. And then guilt for thinking that. So, yes, I do know.'

Did she have to sound so bloody reasonable? And so disappointed with him? Couldn't she cut him some slack? It was all too much, too new, too raw. He tried to breath, struggled. Paced across the room and back, swallowed the lump blocking his throat, and strove for control. Back and forth across his office, which got smaller with every turn. He needed to get out of there, get some air. Stop thinking for a bit to give his mind time to settle down and absorb everything he'd learned over the last few minutes.

'I'm going for a walk.' He headed for the door.

Jodi was out of her chair and in his face so fast he hadn't even reached for the door handle. 'I'm coming with you.'

'No, Jodi. Give me a break here, okay? I need time to myself. It's not like you've given me a weather forecast

or told me the cat's got fleas. This is huge. I need to absorb it all before I decide what I'm going to do.'

Her lips tightened. 'I understand. It's been a big shock.
But I'm coming with you. You'll have plenty of questions
once you start getting past the initial disbelief and I want
to be there to answer them.' When he narrowed his eyes
at her she added quickly, 'I won't say a thing unless you
ask me to.'

Maybe this really was a lookalike Jodi.

His phone sang a tune. He groaned as he read the message. 'Samantha's wondering why I haven't turned up at
the party yet.'

If looks could kill, he'd be a goner. Holding his hands
up in a placating gesture, he added, 'I'm definitely not
in the mood for a party now.' Probably never would be
again. His finger pressed the 'off' button. Shocking how
quickly life could change.

'Samantha is?'

'Not my girlfriend.' He hauled the door open and Jodi
slipped out right alongside him. She stuck to him all the
way through the hospital corridors, through the car park
and onto the street, where he strode blindly along the
footpath, trying to outrun this nightmare.

And, true to her word, she didn't utter a word.

Which was even more disturbing. He did not know
this Jodi at all.

Jodi shivered in the chill night air. Wrapping her arms
around her upper body, she tripped along beside Mitch.

Engrossed in thought, he didn't seem to realise she
was still with him, which gave her a chance to study him
uninterrupted. Every time they passed under a streetlight
she saw the raw shock still in his face. And the serious
bent of his gaze. The clenched jaw.

At least he wasn't shucking Jamie off like a used coat. That had to be good. Mitch was the champion of avoidance when it came to getting close to someone. He knew all the moves to keep people at arm's length. Even in the best times they had together she'd known she had no future with him, that eventually he'd be gone.

That had made it a little easier to toss him out. Only a very little. The weeks and months following that disastrous day had been hard. Learning she was pregnant had added to her grief, but hadn't broken her resolve to stay away from him after the conversation she'd overheard between him and his twin.

'Here, put this on.' Mitch shrugged out of his jacket and handed it to her.

'Th-thanks. Wh-what about y-you?' Her teeth hurt as they chattered from the cold.

'I'll be fine.'

The jacket came down to her knees and she could've wrapped it around herself twice. 'A-anything y-you want to ask m-me?'

'What field did you finally qualify in? Paediatrics or general practice?'

Okay, not about Jamie, then. 'I opted for general practice when I learned I was pregnant.'

'Why?'

As warmth seeped into her chilled muscles she concentrated on telling him what he wanted to know. 'I didn't like the idea of the horrendous hours that working in a hospital entailed. I wanted to be home at the end of the day for my child. Turned out it was a good move. Since Jamie became ill I've only worked part time.' Very part time, some weeks.

'Do you like being a GP?'

Still avoiding the real issue. She sighed. Maybe this

was the way to the heart of the matter, giving him time to assimilate everything. 'I love it. I see the same people regularly, get to know their families, watch the children growing.' Her words dwindled away as she thought of Jamie and how he didn't seem to grow at all these days. How a good day for him was one without pain or not being admitted to hospital.

'Yeah, I can see you fitting right in there. You always could empathise with people as easily as breathing.'

Whereas he'd never enjoy spending his days working with the same people, getting to know their strengths and weaknesses, having them believe they had a connection with him beyond a fifteen-minute consultation. But she took the compliment, held it in her heart; a small warmth in an otherwise frosty situation. 'You obviously still love the adrenalin rush of emergency medicine, though the hours seem to have taken their toll if that little snooze I witnessed is anything to go by.'

His elbows dug into his sides briefly. 'Caught. But in defence I've been working for ten days straight. And before you say it, I haven't changed in that respect. I do love the rush and drama of ED.'

Had he changed at all? In what ways? She hadn't noticed anything different yet. 'What about being HOD? More paperwork, less action, surely?' Definitely not his forte.

'Not in my department. Head of Department isn't a job to be turned on and off. The paper stuff gets done when it gets done, which lands me in hot water too often. Tough. The patients come first. The work's demanding and absorbing. How many people can say they get a buzz out of their job every single day? Do you?'

No, sometimes she was so tired after sitting up all night with Jamie it took everything she had to even turn up. 'I used to love the buzz when I was training in hospital too, but I never let it take over my whole life.' Ouch. Snippy. Settle down. Antagonising the guy wouldn't win her any favours. 'Sorry.'

Mitch stopped and took her elbow to turn her. Looking down into her eyes, he smiled tiredly. 'I guess we've got a few bones to pick over. But maybe not tonight, eh?'

Staring through the half-light, she could see how confused, lost even, he looked. Yet his hand on her elbow was reassuring. Standing here with Mitch, something she'd never thought she'd do again, a sense of homecoming washed over her. The strength she'd loved in him, the gentleness, the caring. She'd missed all that and more.

They might never become real friends, might always bicker and try to avoid each other, but he knew about Jamie now. So nothing would ever be the same for her again, ever be as bad as the last lonely, heartbreaking three years had been. Mitch was back in her life, no matter how tentatively. As if he'd ever truly left. Reaching up, she palmed his bristly chin for an instant. 'You're right. Not tonight.'

In silence they continued along the footpath, dodging Saturday night revellers outside The Shed, a bar that appeared to be very popular. After half an hour they started back towards the hospital and her car. With growing exasperation Jodi waited for Mitch to ask her something, anything, about Jamie. Surely his head was full of questions? Didn't he want to know what Jamie's favourite food was? What toys he loved to play with? Did he take after his father or his mother in temperament?

Mitch would've seen from the photo how physically alike he and his son were. That had been hard at times. There had been days she'd looked at Jamie and cried for Mitch. Not only to be with her, supporting her, sharing the agony of watching her boy getting sicker and sicker, but because she'd missed him so much.

There'd been times when she'd seen Mitch in her son's face and had wanted to charge up to Auckland to tear him apart, to rant and yell at him for being so neglectful of her that she hadn't been able to tell him about his child.

But now the silence hung between them and she didn't know how to break it without upsetting him and she'd already done that in bucketloads tonight. But surely he wanted to know about Jamie's illness and what lay ahead?

They reached the car park and she thought Mitch was going to walk away from her without another word. Anger rolled through her. That wasn't going to happen. 'Mitchell, you can't avoid this one.'

His jaw jutted out, his eyes flashed as angrily as hers must be doing. 'Where is Jamie? Did you bring him to Auckland with you?'

What? 'Like I'd leave my seriously ill child behind while I came up here? Who do you think I am? I'm a very responsible mother, and you'd better believe that.' The words fired out at him and there were plenty more coming, except he put a finger to her lips.

'Hey, stop it. You wanted questions yet when I ask one you take my head off.' Those blue eyes were so reasonable it infuriated her.

She took a deep breath, stamped on her temper and tried for calmness. 'This hasn't been easy, coming to see you.'

'I'm sure it hasn't, but that's also kind of sad. I'd have thought we were better than that.' His gaze remained steady. 'So where is this lad?'

'With Mum in a motel down the road at Greenlane.' She named the motel and reluctantly smiled when he whistled.

'That's a bit trashy, isn't it?'

'Money's tight. And before you say anything, that's not a hint. I hope to find a small flat in the next few days. The hospital did offer to put us up in one of those homes they provide for families with sick children but I don't think I can cope with living with other people, strangers, right now.'

Mitch studied his feet for so long she wondered if he'd fallen asleep standing upright.

'Mitch?'

He didn't look up. 'I'd like to see him.'

Yes. Her hands clenched. Yes, yes. Fantastic. 'Any time you like. We can go there now. The motel's only ten minutes away.'

Lifting his head he drilled her with his gaze. 'Whoa, slow down. Tomorrow will be fine. Let's leave Jamie to his sleep tonight.'

Mitch was right. But wait until tomorrow and he might change his mind. All those hours to come up with reasons not to see his son. 'Are you sure?'

'Yes.' Then, 'What's your plan for seeing specialists?'

'We've got an appointment with a renal specialist on Monday morning. Lucas Harrington. Know him?'

'Yes, a little. An American who moved here with his Kiwi wife a year ago. He's about the best you can get anywhere.'

'That's what I've been told. I also researched him on the internet and liked what I saw. He's written some interesting papers.' But could he save her boy?

'What time on Monday?'

'Huh?'

'Your appointment. I'll come with you. It might help if he knows I'm in the background.'

Her jaw dropped. She hadn't seen that coming. Mitch

might not be owning up to fatherhood yet but he was supporting her in the one way he'd be utterly confident. 'Um, great. Yes, that's wonderful. Thank you. Ten o'clock.'

'Your enthusiasm's overwhelming. I thought this was why you knocked on my door,' he grumbled, then gave her a genuine smile for the first time since she'd walked into his office.

As far as smiles went it wasn't huge or exciting or welcoming, but it was warm and sincere. And her mouth dried. Her empty stomach sucked in. She'd once fallen in love with that smile.

I can't afford to do that again.

But it was going to be good seeing Mitch occasionally over the next few months while Jamie hopefully got the treatment he needed.

'There's something you should know.' Mitch's drawl broke into her thoughts. 'That party I'm supposed to be at? It's an early farewell party. My farewell. I leave for Sydney in less than two months' time, where I've accepted a job in the city's busiest hospital. It's a very prestigious position.'

She gasped, 'I don't believe it. You can't.' Shock rippled through her. Gripping her fists under her chin, she stared up at this man who seemed to slip out of tricky situations more easily than a greased eel slid from a man's hands. 'Of all the things you could've told me, I'd never have picked that one.'

'Bad timing, isn't it? Really bad.'

Her mouth fell open and she gaped at him.

He did sound apologetic. That didn't help one iota.

She almost cried. 'You have no idea.' *What have I done? Can I undo it? How totally unfair it would be to introduce Jamie to his dad only to have Mitchell disappear on him. No, that could not happen. No way.*

Mitch looked directly at her, fixing her with those intense blue eyes. 'It's not right for a child to lose parents at an early age. Better not to have known them at all.'

By the time she found her voice and could get a sound out around the rock in her throat Mitch was long gone.

From the corner of the car park Mitch watched Jodi drive away from the hospital, his heart knocking and his head spinning.

Jodi Hawke had come to town, bringing with her problems he'd never expected to have to face.

'I'm a father.'

Heading for his four-wheel drive in the underground park, he tried to think what this meant to him. Was he thrilled? Excited? Terrified? Angry?

Damn it. He'd go to Samantha's party, drink a tankful and sink into oblivion. Forget Jodi was here. Forget the bombshell she'd dropped.

And how's that going to look in front of your staff? Their HOD off his face at the party they'd put on to say farewell to him? A farewell he couldn't look forward to anymore. Staff who expected better of him.

'I'm a father.'

Yeah, he got that. Sort of. When would it really kick in? To the point where everything he did or thought had to take into consideration a small person? It might never happen with him. He wasn't exactly qualified to be a parent.

Turning, he headed back to the road. The Shed Bar would be crowded and heaving but he could get a drink and not be able to hear himself think. Perfect.

Or he could change into his gym gear, which was in the back of his vehicle, and go for a run up at Auckland Domain. Build up a sweat and tire his body so that it would go to sleep when he finally crawled into bed. Pound the paths that circled the museum.

Yeah, and probably break an ankle tripping over a kerb.

Anyway, he liked the bar idea better. Shoving his hands deep into his trouser pockets, he headed for bourbon. On the rocks.

CHAPTER FOUR

'MUMMY, WHY DO the sheep smell funny?' Jamie leaned through the fence wire peering at the animals grazing on the lush green grass.

Jodi forced a grin but couldn't keep the weariness out of it. 'That's their woolly coat. It keeps them warm and dry, like your jersey does for you. That's made out of sheep's wool too.'

Jamie's brow furrowed as he looked from his fire-engine-red top to the muddy sheep. 'Are there red sheep, Mummy?'

'No, the wool is coloured with red dye, like I did with the icing for your birthday cake. Remember?' Rubbing her eyes with the back of her hand, she stifled another yawn.

What with Mitch's bombshell about Sydney and all the questions buzzing around her head, she hadn't slept a wink last night. Worse, with her mother sleeping in the main room and Jamie in the small bedroom, she hadn't been able to get up and read to distract herself. So Mitch had dominated her mind all night long. Nothing new, really. He'd been dominating it ever since she'd made the decision to move north. Come on, he'd never really left. Mitch had always held a place in her heart. They might be over as far as a loving, sexual relationship went, but she'd never been able to completely let him go. She'd loved him deeply. Missed him more than she'd believed possible.

'Mummy, that man's looking at me.'

She knew. Just knew it was Mitchell. Despite everything that had gone down between them last night, she'd known he'd come. Despite him saying a child shouldn't have to lose a parent, she knew he wouldn't be able to ignore Jamie for long.

Turning slowly, warily, she studied the man standing twenty metres away, who looked as though he didn't know what to do next. 'Hello, Mitch.' He looked so... bewildered. Which was totally unlike him. What would it be like to hold him again? To feel that chest under her cheek? To have his arms around her? Darn, she'd missed him. Really, deep inside missed him.

'Hi, Jodi.' His eyes were glued on Jamie as he slowly closed the gap between them. 'I called in at the motel and Alison told me I'd find you here.'

Mum had probably told him a whole heap more than that. 'Cornwall Park's the perfect place for a small boy who's bored and feeling chained up in a motel unit the size of a gnat's house. All this acreage, the sheep, trees—it's wonderful. I'm going to take him up One Tree Hill shortly.'

Shut up, Jodi. Let Mitch speak. Let him tell you why he's here. Has he come to meet Jamie? Or to explain more about why he's soon heading to Sydney? As if she didn't know the answer to that one. A very prestigious position. One to rub his brother's face in, she'd bet. The guy couldn't stay still if there was an outside chance of getting one over Max.

They were both the same, had a gene that kept them moving on through anything life handed them that hinted at commitment to another person. They couldn't even front up to each other and admit their feelings. And who knew what those were? Mitch and Max probably didn't have a clue. Kind of sad when they were the only close family either of them had.

And now, when she'd turned up with his son, Mitch had got lucky. Or was that nearly lucky? He'd already made plans to go away. Mitch's heart must be doing leaps in the air. Timing was everything. What if she'd been a month earlier? Two months? He'd have immediately started searching for another position far away. Wouldn't he? Or was she justifying her actions again?

'Mummy?' Jamie's little hand crept into hers, his fingers twining tight around her thumb.

She dropped to her haunches, drew her baby into her arms. To protect him? Or herself? From what? 'It's okay, love. He's a…' Swallow. She looked over her son's head at the man who'd helped her create him. 'This is Mitchell, a friend of Mummy's.' Define friend. Define Mitchell Maitland. Impossible right now. Pulling her head away from Jamie, Jodi looked up into the bleak blue gaze of her boy's father. 'Mitch, I'd like you to meet my son, Jamie.' She slowly turned Jamie to face him, holding his frail body against her.

Mitch blanched. She'd hit a tender spot. Tough. This was a battle. If he was about to disappear she wasn't going to introduce him as Daddy. That might antagonise him, and her son's life depended on Mitchell coming onside. She'd do whatever it took to save Jamie. So, Mitch, you're toast. She pushed Jamie forward. 'Shake hands with Mitch like Mummy showed you.'

Her heart swelled with pride and pain as she watched Jamie trot across the space to this man he'd never met, holding out his right hand in greeting. So trusting, so totally unaware how important Mitch could be to him.

Who he was. Until now Jamie had never asked about his father, but it wouldn't be much longer before he started noticing he didn't have one.

'Hello, I'm Jamie Hawke.'

Thankfully Mitch reciprocated. She'd have killed him if he hadn't.

'Hello, young man.' Mitch's hand swallowed his son's for a brief shake. Then it was as though he couldn't let go. Like his hand had frozen in place around Jamie's. 'I'm Mitchell Maitland, but you can call me…' He blinked, swallowed hard. 'Call me Mitch, like your mummy does.'

'Okay.' Jamie tugged his hand free. 'Want to see the sheep with me, Mitch?'

Mitch looked stunned at how easily he'd been accepted. 'Um, all right, I guess.'

But as Jamie ran towards the fence Mitch remained fixed to the spot, studying him. 'He's small for his age, isn't he? And so pale. All part of the renal failure, I know. Does he suffer a lot of pain? Headaches? What's his urine output like?'

Jodi took his arm and led him across to join Jamie. Again Mitch was dealing with this the only way he knew how. But that didn't explain the tremor running up his arm. 'He has intermittent bone pain, lots of headaches, urinary tract infections are a regular occurrence, and there's a score of other symptoms. He also has a sense of humour, loves chicken nuggets and fries, prefers orange juice to fizzy drinks, and wants to be a fireman when he grows up.'

'Not a doctor, then?' A wry smile tweaked Mitch's mouth.

'They're boring. Anyway, I think he's had his fill of medics for a while.'

'That makes sense. Poor little guy. Of all the crappy things to happen to him.'

Jodi pursed her mouth. 'I know. I've spent hours berating the fact *my* boy got sick, but as a doctor I know better than that.'

'I guess if there's anything to be grateful about it is that you are a doctor.' When her eyebrows lifted he grimaced. 'Doesn't make the slightest bit of difference?'

'Not a jot. Sometimes I think it's worse. I've always known what's ahead, and probably spend too much time looking for symptoms that aren't there. Yet.'

Mitch astonished her by dragging her into a hug. His chin rested on her head as he said, 'Jamie's very lucky to have you as his mum. I can't think of anyone else I'd want looking out for my child. To love him, cherish and care for him.'

Blimey. That was so unexpected. But then again, this was one of the charming Maitland twins. Of course he'd know exactly what to say to make her feel good.

Hang on. Was that a kiss on her head? Couldn't be. Not from Mr Enjoy 'em and Leave 'em. But they were in an odd situation. Maybe he was starting to see the whole picture, not just the *Oh, my God, I'm a dad* bit. She'd take it to be a kiss, a kiss given in friendship. And hope she was right.

'Mummy, I want a hug too.'

'Coming right up, my man.' Turning out of Mitch's arms, she leaned down to pick up her boy and hugged him tight. And got the shock of her life when Mitch's arms wrapped around both of them. A giant step forward?

Suddenly Mitch stepped back, his face inscrutable. 'I'll see you tomorrow at the appointment.' He spun on his highly polished shoes and almost ran to his four-wheel drive.

'That went well. Not,' Jodi muttered under her breath as she watched his rapid retreat. 'What next? Huh, Mitch? What am I supposed to do if you don't want to face this?'

Confusion boiled up in her head. If he was going to Australia soon, why had he made an effort to meet Jamie this morning? Had he decided to take an active part in Jamie's life? Or was he just doing what he thought was the right thing? Putting in a cursory appearance? Maybe the reality of meeting Jamie had proved too hard to deal with. Now that he'd seen and met Jamie there was no denying he was a father. So why had he taken off as though a swarm of bees had been after him?

Could it be that—and the breath stuck painfully in her lungs—he'd thought the whole renal failure situation through and realised what she was hoping for?

Then again, last night when he'd told her about Sydney, she'd been unable to hide her anger and disappointment at him leaving—just when he'd found out about Jamie. He'd been ambivalent, saying he thought she'd done the right thing unless it was going to stress Jamie even more. At that point he had still been grasping the fact he was a father, nothing else. Of course Mitch leaving would cause Jamie grief. He mightn't ask why he didn't have a father yet, but to learn he had one only to lose him almost immediately would certainly create problems.

And right now she and Jamie didn't need any more of those. They already had more than their share.

Except there were more. Her unexpected need for Mitch, for one. It sprang up at her in full force, denying the difficulties lying between them, ignoring the fact that Mitch Maitland would never settle down in one place for longer than necessary, pushing aside the number of times he'd left her waiting. The fact was he was undeniably as gorgeous as ever. He'd be very easy to fall in love with all over again. Big problem, that.

Three attempts and the key still wouldn't fit into the ignition. Not surprising when Mitch's head was in turmoil. He wanted to vent his frustration, to shout at the damned thing and bang the steering wheel with his clenched fist. Why did he feel such a strong yearning for that child out there in Jodi's arms?

No ordinary child. His son. Where had this sense of belonging come from when most of his life he'd been happy to believe he didn't want kids of his own? It had arrived, bam, the moment he'd seen Jamie standing by the fence, his little face puckered in wonder as he'd watched the sheep.

Was this how a father felt when the midwife handed him his baby for the very first time? Couldn't be. That would be more poignant, seeing the birth, holding the brand-new baby. Or would it?

When he'd decided to follow Jodi to Cornwall Park he'd believed he was prepared to see Jamie. He'd spent most of the night thinking about him. And about why Jodi hadn't told him earlier. And about Jodi herself. Part of him still didn't want to believe that the rumpled-looking woman now heading for her rental car was the vivacious, fashion-conscious lady he'd once lived with.

'Damn it.' His hand unclenched, clenched again. He'd thought he'd just meet the boy and be able to remain impervious to him—at least until he'd worked out what he was going to do. But that first glimpse had brought reality crashing down on him like a load of bricks. Shock and fear had fought with something like pride as he'd stood drinking in the unbelievable sight of the small boy who had his genes. The kid was beautiful, cute.

And so bloody sick. His heart squeezed tight. His fingers gripped the key. Inside his head a drum began beating a steady rhythm. Jamie. Bang. His son. Bang. Jodi. Bang. On and on it went.

Nothing Jodi had said had prepared him for what he'd seen when he'd studied Jamie. He knew sick kids, dealt with them daily. But this was his boy. Jodi had done the right thing, bringing him to see Lucas Harrington. The man was the best in his field in New Zealand, and close to it on the world stage. He had access to other top specialists too, including Max Maitland, transplant surgeon extraordinaire.

His teeth were grinding and he swore under his breath. Max was going to love this. He could see his brother's eyes lighting up now at the thought of Mitch needing something from him. Worse, somehow he had to tell Max about Jamie and his illness. How did he do that when they rarely talked? On the occasions they had to work together with a patient they were very professional. Thankfully, they didn't cross paths too often, though when they did there wasn't a civil word spoken between them. But all that was about to change. Jamie would be Max's patient.

Angrily shoving any thoughts of his brother aside, he concentrated on Jodi and her telling *him* he was a father. Had that been the right thing to do? Of course it was. He had two healthy kidneys. That had to be the biggest motivator for Jodi. His kidney—for Jamie. Anger should be enveloping him. She'd manipulated him. Perfectly. So was he going to follow the path she'd mapped out for him? He shrugged. Too soon to know yet. He still had to get his head around being a parent.

Across the road Jodi was buckling Jamie into a child's car seat. Her body was bent at the waist, her long legs seeming to go on for ever. His body tensed as memories of caressing those legs with the satin skin, of kissing his way from her knees to the apex where her womanhood waited, warm and moist, for him.

He shoved the key hard. Finally got it into the ignition. The engine roared as his heavy foot hit the accelerator. The wheels spun as he pulled away.

Jodi raised a startled face as he passed. A shocked, sad face with disappointment blinking out at him. That Jodi he remembered without any trouble at all.

Jodi Hawke, the woman who always sneaked into his skull in that still hour before the sun lightened night into day. Reminding him of what he'd lost.

Huh, you didn't lose Jodi. You handed her an excuse to leave you and then felt hard done by.

Forget those emotions. Forget why she'd suddenly turned up with Jamie. He wasn't ready to contemplate that can of worms. Not today.

Strange how already he felt some strange connection with the lad, as though there was a thread running between them. Which was frightening. Terrifying. But he was leaving for Sydney soon. That concerned him too. One thing he was an expert on was living without his father. He took a glance into the rental car as he drove past. 'My boy.'

That thread connecting them was tightening, pulling him inexorably closer to the kid, no matter how far away he drove. As though genes cut through all the words to the heart of the matter. If he hadn't felt so wired, confused and downright terrified, he'd laugh at himself because never once had he envisaged this moment. He'd sworn he'd leave children and parenting to the rest of the human race.

Driving through the park, he watched out for Sunday

strollers and kids chasing each other, more aware than ever before of those children and the dangers they placed themselves in as they played.

What was it like to play ball with your son? To help him get dressed in the morning? To read him bedtime stories? His head swirled with images of him and Jamie together. Alien images, but kind of intriguing and warm and nice as well. Damn it.

And in every picture flicking across his brain was Jodi. The real Jodi or the lookalike Jodi? The woman he'd once thought he might love? Or a complete stranger?

He needed to know. Now. Before he could digest anything more about that child and what to do for him. He had to find his Jodi amongst all those heart-wrenching emotions continually scudding across her beautiful face.

Lifting his foot, he slowed and turned back the way he'd come, pulled up behind her car. Climbing out, he went to meet her just as she hauled the driver's door open to get in.

'Mitch?' She tilted her head back, blinking as the autumn sunlight caught her eyes.

'I need to find you.' He tapped her sternum with a finger. 'Somewhere in there is the Jodi I once knew.' And then he took her shoulders and pulled her close. His lips covered hers as she gasped. Hot air spilled into his mouth. But he didn't pull away. Instead, he eased into her, hauling her up close against his chest, his stomach, his thighs. And tasted her, recognised her. This was his Jodi. Not that worried woman holding him to ransom. This warm, responsive woman not pushing him away but sliding her hands around his neck—that was the real Jodi.

He breathed her in. She still used lavender-scented shampoo. His hands splayed over her waist. His tongue danced across hers. Finally everything was beginning to make sense. This was the real deal.

Which meant so were all the problems she'd brought to town with her.

Jodi watched Mitch's vehicle until it was lost from sight behind the oak trees lining the park roads. Her finger traced her lips. 'What just happened?'

Worse. Why had she let it happen?

No. Worse was that she'd enjoyed the kiss. More than enjoyed it, had felt it was right. It made her feel she'd finally come home, come in from the cold.

Which was so stupid because it didn't solve a thing. Their son was still ill. Mitch was still leaving for Sydney. She still didn't have a clue what came after Jamie's transplant.

Slumping against the car, she couldn't stop the warmth creeping through where her body had been chilled for weeks. Mitch had said he hadn't recognised her until he'd kissed her.

'Why? Have I changed that much?'

Must have. But she liked Mitch's technique for finding her. Except it would probably complicate things even more to have that kiss hanging over them.

No, the complication came from the fact that she'd enjoyed it, hadn't wanted Mitch to stop.

This was not what she'd come to Auckland for.

Or was it? Deep down in that dark corner had she been hoping for a reunion with Mitch? A kiss-and-make-up, fairy-tale ending to the years of anguish?

'If that's what you're wanting, you're in deep water. Mitch is still on the run from himself. You're going to get left behind and be angry at him for that when it will be your own fault for even thinking you could make it work again.'

Straightening up, Jodi turned and opened the car door again. Peeking in the back, she saw Jamie was dozing. At least he wouldn't have seen that kiss. Did it matter if he had?

Who knew? He might accept Mitch more readily if he thought Mummy liked this new man who had started hanging around a bit.

What Jamie wouldn't understand was that Mummy more than liked him, had always more than liked him.

Time to head back to the motel and put Jamie to bed for an hour. But as she drove slowly along the road the thought of that dark, cold unit did not excite her. At the intersection she looked left and right. To heck with it. She'd head for One Tree Hill. If Jamie stayed asleep then he was getting his nap anyway. If he woke up she'd show him the sights of Auckland.

And try to push that kiss down into the dark hole where all her other great Mitch memories were stored, gathering dust.

At the top of the hill she parked and went to sit on the stone wall where she could see Jamie and yet have the fresh air blowing around her cobweb-filled head. She tried not to think about anything.

But that kiss had startled her, not to mention it had quickly awoken a need inside that she doubted would be easily ignored.

Cars came and went, disgorging tourists who talked in many languages as they pointed out landmarks to each other. When Jamie grizzled she went and freed him from the seat belt and lifted him down to the pavement.

'Let me carry him.' Mitch stood in front of her, wariness in those unsettling eyes.

'That's the second time in less than an hour you've sneaked up on me.' There was a wobble in her voice that annoyed her.

'It wasn't intentional. Either time.' He reached down for Jamie. 'Hey, sport. Want to see Auckland?'

She followed slowly, wondering why he'd returned. She had no idea. It was as though he was on an elastic rope, pinging back and forth. Now she saw him. Now she didn't. Now she did.

At the wall, Jamie stood on the top so he could see the city sprawled out below. Gripping her jacket, he asked, 'What's that over there, Mummy?'

'That's the harbour bridge,' she told him, hoping they were looking at the same thing. 'And that skinny tall building with a knob on top is the Sky Tower.'

'Can I go up there?' Jamie asked.

'When you're a bit bigger.' *When you can go alone and I don't have to suffer vertigo.*

'Why do I have to be big?'

'It's a Mummy rule.'

'That works?' Rare amusement laced Mitch's question.

'On a good day.' She tried to smile back and managed some sort of twist to her mouth.

His amusement faded, replaced by seriousness. 'Why did you come to Auckland? Was it only so Jamie could get the best medical care? Or did you come for my undivided attention and support? Hoping I'd drop everything to be by your side now that you've decided to tell me I'm a parent?'

Jodi flinched. And considered his questions. He had every right to ask. 'Both reasons.' She paused, thought it through some more. This was too important to muck up. There was a third reason, the most important one. But she was afraid to bring that out into the cold light of day yet. More than that, she'd prefer Mitch to broach it first. 'At least I think so.'

'Explain.'

I'm trying, without pushing you too hard. 'From the moment I heard about Lucas Harrington, nothing would've kept me from bringing Jamie to see him. At first I thought that's all it would be—a visit. Maybe a few visits, depending on the outcome of the consultation. Then back to Dunedin while we waited to see what could be done.' She rubbed Jamie's back absentmindedly. 'You've got to understand that Jamie comes first, second and third with me. Whatever's important for him is important for me. Nothing and no one will get in the way of that.' *Not even you. Despite that bone-melting kiss.*

'I'd never doubt it. You've always had the right instincts when it comes to other people so you'd be no different with your own child.'

So what did he doubt? That her altruistic claims regarding his role were false? 'I was wrong not to tell you I was pregnant. It was wrong not to let you know we had a son. But at the time it felt like the right thing to do for me. I can't change that.'

'I'm happy to let it drop, Jodi. As you say, we can't undo anything.'

Astonishment caught her. Blinking back sudden tears—darn, but there were a lot of those this weekend—she leaned over and kissed his cold cheek. 'Thank you.'

Together they stared out over the city, Jodi wrapping her arms around Jamie for added warmth. Then she gave Mitch a little more of herself. 'When Dad went to prison, Mum worked every hour of the day and night, trying to get ahead, trying to prove to the townspeople she could be a success and that Dad's criminal habits hadn't rubbed off on her. I really didn't factor into her plans in any way other than as a child to be fed, clothed and educated.' She paused, added quietly, 'I know Mum loved—loves me. But it was a lonely, cold way to grow up. She was never there for me. I didn't want sandwiches. I wanted hugs and mother-daughter talks.'

'Did you think I'd act in a similar way with my child?' There was no condemnation in his voice, only a need to know. Which was kind of sad.

Yet she couldn't keep the bitterness out of her voice. It had been collecting for a long time. 'And wouldn't you have? Isn't that why we broke up? You were always too busy for me. I was like your car: handy when needed otherwise best left parked up. Not the sort of man I wanted for Jamie's father.' But she could've dealt with that if only she'd given him a chance.

'That night of your birthday I was dealing with an emergency and couldn't get away.' He ground out the words.

'Mitch, you could never get away. There were always emergencies. There were other doctors available. You didn't try hard enough. You didn't even consider that a text to say you weren't going to make it would be preferable to leaving me sitting in the middle of the restaurant while I copped pitying looks from all the other diners.'

'I was pushing you.'

'I don't understand.'

'Like a test. Waiting, watching for your breaking point, which to me was inevitable. The closer we got, the harder I pushed.'

'So I passed the test with flying colours. And in doing so failed you.' And me. It was all beginning to make sense at last. If only she'd known more about Mitch's insecurities back then, how different the last three years might've been.

'Mummy, I'm cold.'

Oh, heck. 'Jamie, love, sorry. We'll go back to the motel now.' She had a lot to think about regarding Mitch and her role in this screwed-up situation.

'Don't want to go to bed. I want chicken nuggets.'

She picked Jamie up and headed for the car.

'Jodi.' Mitch spoke softly as he opened the door for her to place Jamie in his car seat. 'You're right. I should've let you know I wasn't going to make it that night. I let it get out of hand. I didn't text or phone and you kicked me out. Over and done. That's history. Since you've turned up again I'd like us to find a way to get along, at least for Jamie's sake, while his health is sorted.'

'And afterwards? Will you want to be around for him? It was you who said it would be better for him not to meet you than to have you walk away later. And yet here you are. Does that mean you want to be a part of his life?'

'Why wouldn't I be?' He had the audacity to look startled.

Something in her head exploded. 'Because I wasn't worth the effort of something as easy as a text so why would I expect more for my son?'

'Don't I deserve a second chance?'

'Aren't I giving you one?'

His hands slid into his pockets and he leaned against the front of the car. 'I'm trying to get my head around it all. Please be patient.'

'Sure.' Her hands fisted in the air between them, her teeth dug into her bottom lip. 'Sure.'

'There's something else that's bugging you, isn't there? Something from the past you're busting to get off your chest.'

How did he know that? How could he read her so well

after all these years? He couldn't read her at all back then. 'Why did you ask me out that first time?'

'Because I wanted your company. I liked you.'

Narrowing her eyes at him, she forced the words out. 'Not because you wanted to show Max you could do better with his old girlfriend than he had?'

Mitch reared back, horror twisting his handsome face. 'Where did you get that crazy idea?'

'I heard you. You and Max, shouting at each other one day when I came around to your flat to tell you I was pregnant. Max yelling that brothers never, ever went out with each other's girlfriends, current or otherwise. You taunting him about how I preferred living with you than him.'

'Sh—'

'Don't swear in front of Jamie,' she snarled. 'There was more. Max taunted you by saying he was surprised you hadn't got me pregnant to prove how much better than him you were.'

'And I told him I didn't intend wrecking my great career because I had duties at home with a family.' Mitchell slammed his hands on his thighs and leaned back, staring up at the clouds scudding across town. His throat worked hard and he swallowed fast. His eyes blinked rapidly. 'That wasn't about you. It was about me. And Max.'

'Of course it was. How stupid of me to think any different. But I'll tell you this for nothing.' She paused for emphasis. 'I don't believe you. I hated being used as a scratching post between you two. I'd liked Max until then. I'd loved you. More than anyone, anything.'

His head snapped up. 'Jodi, no, you didn't.' His face lost its tanned look as all colour drained away. 'You couldn't have.' There was a tremor in his voice.

She shook her head, afraid to say anything more in

case she really tore him apart to the point of no return. She'd said too much already. Her temper had got the better of her at the worst possible moment. She'd held that hurt in for so long now that a few more weeks wouldn't have mattered. But, no, she'd opened her mouth and slapped him over the head with her words.

'Maybe Max said that to me because he cared deeply for you, and when I picked up with you he saw red.'

Her chin dropped a little as she contemplated that. 'No, he didn't. It was Max who called our relationship off.' Not that she'd been broken-hearted. They had got on well but she hadn't been in love with the guy. And he certainly hadn't loved her.

'He's a Maitland, remember?'

'A commitment dodger?'

'Yeah, exactly.' Mitch's sigh hurt her.

'You're wrong. Max and I got on okay but there was no chemistry. None at all. We should never have dated for as long as we did. It became a comfortable habit, really.'

Mitch's eyes widened. 'Truly?' When she nodded he continued. 'Still, you should never have heard that particular argument. It was pure Max and Mitch vitriol, each trying to hurt the other. You know how good at that we are.' He drew a breath. 'And I swear the only reason I asked you out that night was because I liked you, was attracted to you and wanted to get to know you better.'

'Oh, okay. Thanks.' She nibbled her lip, trying to ignore the elephant between them. She'd loved Mitch. And now he knew. 'I had hoped we'd had more going for us than your antipathy towards your brother.'

'Jodi, we had much more. My problems with Max never had anything to do with why I was with you. For me it was all about you and me.'

She'd put it behind her. She had to. For Jamie. And maybe even for herself. 'Let's go feed our boy.'

Let's forget my tongue has a mind of its own sometimes. She slapped at her cheeks. When would this watery stuff dry up? She never did tears. Yeah, sure.

CHAPTER FIVE

MONDAY MORNING WAS grey and wet. The clouds oozed drizzle. It suited Jodi's mood.

'You sure you don't want any toast?' Mum asked for the fourth time.

Jodi shook her head, irritated by her mother's persistence. 'I wouldn't be able to keep it down.' Even the tea she'd drunk sat like a puddle in her stomach. She wanted to be at the hospital now, meeting Lucas Harrington, getting to the nitty-gritty of Jamie's medical issues. But it was barely gone seven-thirty.

'Want me to do anything with Jamie?'

'Thanks, Mum, but I'll leave him for as long as possible. He had a bad night.' Which meant so had she. There was grit in her eyes, a dull throb in the base of her skull, and her limbs were lead-lined.

'Then I'll take the dirty clothes down to a laundry I saw when I went for a walk yesterday. I can take my laptop with me and do some work while I wait.' Mum started stuffing Jamie's clothes into a plastic shopping bag.

'Thanks, Mum. I do appreciate it.' More than that, she really loved it that her mum had come up to Auckland with them, even if only for the first few days. It had made all the difference, being able to leave Jamie with her while she'd gone in search of Mitch. Mum's support was always practical, and she'd come to recognise it for what it was—love.

'Jamie's my concern, too.'

Mum seemed to make more time for him than she'd ever done for *her*. In fact, since they'd learned about Jamie's kidney disorder Mum had changed, putting more effort into helping her, being there to give her a break, and sometimes offering to pay the overdue bills. As she hated parting with her hard-earned money, that was huge. Despite being wealthy due to her own hard work, she hadn't learned to relax. Work had been her saviour, money her prize.

Jodi jumped. Someone was knocking on the door. Opening it, she gasped, 'Mitch. What are you doing here?'

'I thought that since I'm going to Jamie's appointment with you I may as well give you a lift to the hospital.'

'But we're not going for more than two hours.' He looked absolutely fabulous in his grey suit and light blue shirt. The darker blue tie matched his eyes perfectly.

A sheepish look crept over his face. 'Is it a problem? I can come back later.'

Was this about Mitch wanting to see Jamie again? Or to make himself useful? She stepped back, holding the door wide. Or did he have things to say to her? 'Come in.'

'I brought breakfast.' He held up a grocery bag. 'Bacon and eggs.'

Nausea swamped Jodi. No way would she be able to hold that down. 'We had toast a little while ago,' she fibbed to save his feelings.

Her mother stood up. 'Bacon and eggs might be good for you, my girl.' She switched her fierce look to Mitch. 'I'm glad you're going with Jodi and Jamie to the specialist. She needs you there. So does Jamie.'

Here we go. Mum had never had any time for the

charming Maitland brothers, always warning her that she'd get into trouble if she hung around with either of them. How true, if having the most gorgeous little boy on the planet was trouble.

Mitch gave Mum one of his serious smiles, wisely withholding one of his charm-filled variety. 'Alison, you're right, which is why I'm here. I will do what I can for Jamie and Jodi over the next couple of months.'

'Okay.' Jodi went for the peace plan. 'Mum, I've got a few things from yesterday that need washing.'

'Where's Jamie?' Mitch asked, before her mother could say anything more to him.

'Dozing in bed. Not a good night. I'll get him up shortly.'

Thankfully, Mum decided to leave well alone and, picking up the laundry, she slung her laptop carry bag over her shoulder and disappeared outside.

Jodi switched the kettle on, more for something to do than the need for a hot drink. She still couldn't get her head around the fact that she was in the same city as Mitch, let alone the same motel room with only an arm's length between them. While she'd lain awake beside Jamie during the night she'd had plenty of time to think about this man who'd once made her heart sing. If only he hadn't been so commitment shy. But he had been, still was, so there was no point in rehashing her old feelings for him.

'Aren't you entertaining a TV crew this week?' she asked, vaguely remembering something that doctor had said in Mitch's office on Saturday night.

'I've been into work already and arranged for Aaron to cover for me this morning. For all his grizzling I think he's stoked to be fronting some of the documentary.'

She gave him a quick grin. 'And you wouldn't be?'

His answering grin was self-deprecating. 'Not at all.'

A cry sounded in the other room. 'Here we go. Jamie doesn't wake up sweetly. Especially after a rough night.' This was sure to send Mitch charging out of the motel faster than an angry bull.

Pulling the curtains open, she sat on the edge of the bed and ran her hand over Jamie's damp hair. 'Hey, sweetheart. It's time to get up and have some breakfast.' She kept talking softly while rubbing his head, then his back, slowly coaxing the crying to a sniffle then to a few hiccups. 'That's my boy. Shall we put your tiger top on today?'

'Okay.'

Really? That easily? Jodi studied Jamie and realised he was looking beyond her to the doorway. A quick glance showed Mitch leaning against the doorframe. That's why she'd won the first round in the dressing stakes so easily. Mitch was a huge distraction.

'Let's get you some toast and honey.' That usually meant Jamie would automatically want cereal.

'Okay, Mummy.'

Blink. Was something wrong with her hearing this morning? Where had this little angel come from? She plopped a kiss on her boy's cheek. Noted the slight temperature from the warmth on his brow. Paracetamol coming up with that toast.

Mitch spoke up. 'Can I put the toast on?'

'Thanks, that would help. I'll give the tiger a face wash.' Swinging Jamie up into her arms, she winced as her back clicked.

'He's heavy for you.' Mitch reached out to Jamie. 'Hi, sport. Can I carry you to the bathroom?'

Jodi held her breath, certain that this gesture would lead to tears, if not tantrums.

Jamie jammed a thumb in his mouth, staring at Mitch

warily. Then he nodded and held his free hand out to him. Stunned, Jodi handed him over to his father. 'Guess I'm on toast duty, then.'

'Ahh, are you sure? What if Jamie doesn't like me washing him?'

'Then I'll be right with you. Coffee?'

When Jamie trotted out to join her a few minutes later Mitch was right behind him, a bewildered smile lighting up his face. 'That was easy.'

Jodi handed him a mug of black coffee. 'Beginner's luck.' But it warmed her heart that he'd done something for Jamie. The first hands-on thing and he'd come out of it with a smile. That had to be good. Didn't it?

'Now, about that breakfast.' Mitch leaned against an impossibly small bench and eyeballed Jodi. 'You could do with feeding up. I don't believe you've had anything. Facing today on an empty stomach is not a good idea.'

'I don't want to carry a rubbish bin around with me either,' she grumped as she elbowed him out of the way to make coffee.

'If I cook it, will you at least try to eat a little?' Mitch slid back against the bench. He wasn't giving up on her that easily. 'I'll carry the bin.'

She glared up at him from under lowered eyebrows. 'Persistent, aren't you?'

'That's a yes, then.' He ignored the flush spreading across her pale cheeks and delved through the two small cupboards to find a pan. 'I can feel your eyes boring holes in my back.' He unpacked the groceries, opened the packet of bacon.

'Which part of no didn't you understand?'

'Which part of persistent don't you?' He turned around and was fixed with a look that told him to back off. A look distinctly lacking in humour. 'Here's the deal. I'll cook some food and if you still don't feel like eating then that's okay with me.'

It wasn't true but he wasn't about to have a big argument over what she ate for breakfast. Somehow he doubted Jodi could take too much angst this morning, even if he was only doing it for her own good.

She dipped her head in acknowledgment. 'Deal.' Those brown orbs were filled with exhaustion, and behind that he saw her need for someone to take care of her, to stand at her side while she faced a new round of specialists today. A need she'd never in a month of birthdays admit to.

'I've told my staff I might not be available for most of the day. I intend spending it with you while we talk to Lucas and anyone else he might refer Jamie to.' Including Max. Damn it. He needed food in his stomach to manage that.

She didn't move, didn't say a word. But her gratitude was in the welling up of tears and the lightening of the brown of her eyes.

If only he could give her everything else she required as easily.

One step at a time, boyo. One step at a time.

Lucas Harrington turned out to be a genial man who immediately won Jodi over by simply spending time getting to know Jamie and putting him at ease. He acted as though he had all the time in the world for her little boy, and yet he had to be extremely busy. The examination he eventually gave Jamie was thorough and gentle.

Jodi nibbled her lip and watched Lucas's face the whole time, looking for clues of what he thought. Not that she expected any nasty surprises: she'd already had them all. But worry held a permanent place in her head when it came to Jamie's health.

Beside her, Mitch picked up her hand and held it in his. His thumb rubbed her wrist, softly, soothingly. When she dared to shift her vigil from Lucas to take a quick peek at Mitch she was surprised to find his eyes fixed on her, concern and care staring out at her. If only she'd had him beside her right from the beginning. It would've been so much better to have someone to share the burden, to talk about Jamie's health and future. But that couldn't be changed. She'd chosen not to tell him. And if he had known, it still wouldn't have changed Jamie's situation.

Mitch whispered, 'Hang in there, Jodi. Jamie's doing fine.'

'He's so brave.' Her teeth nibbled her already tender bottom lip. 'If only I could swap places with him. It's so not fair.'

'I think you're very brave too. I'm only beginning to understand what it's been like for you, and I'm probably so far off the mark but, hell, Jodi, you're a marvel.'

'I'm a mother. It comes with the territory. And I wouldn't have it any other way.'

Understanding filled his gaze. His thumb stilled on her wrist. Then he lifted her hand and kissed her palm. 'Thank you from me for Jamie.'

Shock rippled through her. What a difference thirty-six hours made. Mitch had gone from denial to acceptance that they had a child together. He'd made her breakfast—which seemed to be staying in place. Now he was sitting with her throughout their appointment, totally supportive. Blimey.

'Right.' Lucas's deep voice blasted through her wonder. 'Let's get Jamie back into his tiger suit and then we'll talk.'

With Jamie dressed and sitting on her knee, Jodi braced herself. She knew what was coming but hearing it from this man would take away her last, futile grain of hope.

Lucas cleared his throat and looked at her. 'I've read all the notes sent up by your specialists in Dunedin and I don't see any reason to disagree with their prognosis.'

Her stomach churned. She tasted bacon at the back of her throat and not a rubbish bin in sight. In a strange, quivery voice she asked the specialist, 'Are you going to run more tests?'

Mitch gripped her hand tight. She gripped back, probably crushing every bone in his.

'I'm going to keep everything to a minimum. Jamie doesn't need any more distress than is absolutely necessary,' Lucas told them.

Jodi liked this gentle man even more.

Tapping his pen against the desk pad, he added, 'But I can't avoid all the tests, I'm afraid. We need to take some bloods.' Tap, tap, tap. 'We need to put him on stronger antibiotics too. I'm sure you're aware of his temperature.'

'That's happened overnight,' she told him. 'Please, just tell me.' Everything. Nothing. Make it all go away.

Lucas's voice was very matter-of-fact. 'Jamie does need a kidney transplant. Urgently.'

She knew that. Had heard it in Dunedin. That's why they were here. But it still caused her breathing to cease, her heart to stop. The truth hurt, like a knife turning in her tummy. Shredding her to bits. Her boy was dying. Slowly, painfully. Horribly. And now she had to depend on someone else volunteering a kidney. Or, worse, another mother losing her child so Jamie could live. She opened her mouth to answer Lucas, but nothing came out. Not one word, not even a sound.

Mitch's hand still held hers, but it was the specialist he spoke to. 'Lucas, do you do the transplant surgery?'

'No. As you are well aware, we have an excellent transplant team here, headed by none other than your brother. I'd prefer that Max does this.'

Beside her Mitch tensed, then shocked her with, 'He is the best.'

Max to do the operation? Jodi could not swallow the lump blocking her throat. Max? Too weird. Too family. But she'd always known it would come to this. 'What about Carleen Murphy? I hear she's very good.'

Lucas studied her so long Jodi knew he had to be seeing right into her head, seeing her confusion, her unwillingness to have Jamie's uncle operate on him. 'You'll be meeting with the whole transplant team. We'll leave deciding who does the operation until afterwards.'

She couldn't ask for better than that.

Mitch wanted to run from the room, to get as far as possible from the kind eyes and disastrous words of Lucas Harrington, to block out the horror. But he couldn't. He'd run out of time. This was when he stood up to be counted. Acted like the strong male he'd always pretended to be.

Unwittingly he looked at Jamie. Another look at the boy with the pale face and the small frame. Wished he hadn't because what he saw made his heart tighten painfully. Surprisingly it continued pumping.

Face the truth. Face what I've been hiding from since Jodi told me about Jamie's illness. This kid needs a new kidney. He'll die without it. And I've only just met him. My flesh and blood. I don't want to lose him before I've got to know him.

I don't want to lose him at all.

My flesh and blood. My kidneys might be compatible.

'Mitch?' Jodi nudged him. 'We're finished with Lucas for now. I need to take Jamie up to the lab.'

He saw the pain for Jamie in her eyes. Saw the way she held on to her son for dear life and knew she wouldn't let him carry Jamie for her. Not now, at this moment, when she'd faced the truth of the situation—again.

'Hell, Jodi, how have you held yourself together through all this?' He wasn't managing very well after one doctor's consultation. Jodi would've had plenty of those. She'd done it all alone. Her mother might've helped but Alison wasn't known for dealing with the emotional stuff when it came to her daughter's needs. Just like him. He could blame the fact he hadn't had long to get used to having a son who was seriously ill, but that was a cop-out.

Jodi might've been right not to want involve him in Jamie's life.

But it was too bloody late. He was involved. Like it or not. And he was coming to like it, horrendous problems or not.

In the corridor she peered at him over the top of Jamie's head, those beautiful, suck-him-in eyes filled with resignation. 'There's never been any choice. Jamie needs me to be strong, to fight his battles, to love him. If I fail he has nobody.'

Time to start thinking about these two, not himself. Mitch swallowed hard. 'He has me. For what it's worth, I accept I'm his father and therefore have a role to play in his life.'

As Jodi's eyes widened in relief he felt a surge of pride. And astonishment. It hadn't hurt a bit to say that. Would that come later when he thought through the consequences? No, actually, he didn't think it would.

You've just taken a giant step forward, boyo.

Then dismay shivered through him, knocking down

the good feeling. What about Sydney and that fabulous job he'd been angling to get for over a year now? Was he prepared to give that away? He hadn't thought about that for a few hours. Relax. Jodi and Jamie could join him over there. After the transplant, of course. Yeah, that would work. Jodi could find work in a general practice if she wanted to, and he'd be able to spend time with Jamie in his downtime. They might even find adjoining apartments somewhere central.

Definitely a solution to everything. For the first time since he'd opened his eyes to find Jodi in his office, things were looking up.

If he ignored the axe hanging over them.

Jamie needed a new kidney. Fast.

And he had one to spare.

As Mitch took her elbow and eased her through the throng of people streaming in the opposite direction, Jodi tried to assimilate the full extent of what he'd just said. Did he understand how big the role of father could be? Why wouldn't he? He'd spent all his adult life avoiding getting into the situation where he'd have to be a dad.

'Mummy, can we go home?' Jamie sniffled against her neck. 'I don't like it here.'

'Oh, sweetheart, I know you don't.' She tried to avoid saying an outright no. 'We'll go back to the motel soon.'

Despite the phlebotomist being so careful and gentle, Jamie had still felt the needle that had drawn his blood. His little face had puckered up with resignation. She'd had a sudden urge to pick him up and run. Run from all the uncertainty, the kind medical staff, the big question of Mitch. Run and hide in a warm place where they could pretend none of this was happening. If Mitch hadn't been there, watching over them like a fierce male protector, she really might've taken off.

'I don't want to go there. I want to go home and see Bambi.'

'Who is Bambi?' Mitch asked.

'My cat.' Jamie's head twisted around as he sought out this man who didn't seem to understand anything.

'A cat named Bambi? That's novel.'

Jodi smiled despite everything. 'Better than Knickers, which is the name of the boy next door's puppy.'

Mitch chuckled. 'I didn't realise there was quite such a wide range of pet names out there. Whatever happened to Socks or Blackie?'

'My cat's not black. He's ginger,' Jamie informed him through a sniff.

'And he is really a she, proof being the litter we found in the bottom of the hall cupboard last month.' Jodi smiled her thanks at Mitch for the diversion. Hopefully they'd got past Jamie's need to go home for a little while longer, at least until they'd collected his prescription and dosed him up.

Mitch asked Jamie, 'Feel like going to the canteen and getting a juice, sport?'

'I think so.'

'What do you say?' Jodi nudged her boy.

'Thank you, Mitch. Are you going to get Mummy a coffee? She likes one when I have a juice.'

'Then, yes, that's what we'll do.' His hand tugged her left along another corridor. 'This way. The canteen shouldn't be too busy at this time of the morning.'

Thankfully Mitch was right. Only a few people sat at the scattered tables. About to give a sigh of relief, Jodi suddenly froze, her feet unable to propel her any further forward as she stared at the man seated in the far corner reading the newspaper as he drank from a mug.

Max Maitland.

She so wasn't ready for this man. She hadn't sorted everything out with Mitch yet, so how could she explain to his twin about Jamie? Because the way these two didn't get on, always tried to outdo the other in absolutely everything, Max was going to want to score points out of her sudden appearance with a child in tow. Mitch. Her head flipped back as she sought his face. But he was staring across the room with the same emotions racing through his eyes as she was feeling.

'Let's go.' She nudged him in the side. 'We can get a juice somewhere else.' Preferably on the other side of the moon.

Mitch turned to propel Jodi out of the canteen. He definitely wasn't ready to have Max learn about his son. Probably never would be, but there'd be no avoiding it. All he asked right at this moment was that they got out of here without being seen so they could go somewhere quiet and discuss how much Max should be told. One day. One whole day, that was all he wanted.

'Why can't I have it now, Mummy?' Jamie's voice rose to a loud squeal. 'You promised.'

Mitch bit down on his frustration. The little guy didn't understand what was going on. 'We'll find a better place, okay?'

'Mitch?' Max called across the room. 'Disappearing before you've even got here?'

Damn. Luck was definitely not on his side today. But maybe it would be better getting this out of the way. Huh. As if. Resigned, Mitch braced himself and tucked Jodi under his arm to turn around with her—and met the startled glower of his brother as he noticed who was with him.

'Jodi? Is that you?' Max unfolded himself from the chair to stand tall, a smile spreading across his handsome face. 'What brings you to town?' Then his eyes widened further still. 'And who's this?'

Mitch felt her tremble but she stepped forward, away from his side. 'Hello, Max. It's good to see you. And this is Jamie, my son.'

Mitch would've laughed if the situation hadn't been so damned serious. Instead he groaned and held his hand tight at his side. Max's jaw had dropped, and for once he seemed lost for words.

Jodi crossed the remaining gap to his brother. 'It's been a long time but you're looking as good as ever.'

She hadn't said that about *him*. Mitch studied the expression in her bold eyes. Aha. She was pandering to Max's ego, softening him up, trying to prevent a tirade of questions. Especially when it was blatantly obvious who Jamie's father had to be. And what was *he* doing about the situation? Letting Jodi down.

'Max, Jamie is also my son.' There were a million things he wanted to add to that bald statement. He and Max had an unvarying pattern to their conversations and arguments, which always included getting one over the other, a power struggle to come out on top. But not today. He couldn't abide Max saying anything wrong about Jodi or Jamie.

Max blinked then drawled, 'Even a blind man could see that.'

Jodi murmured, 'Strong Maitland genes.'

Then Max got his second wind. 'Jodi, it's great to see you. Really. I've wondered what happened to you.' And the guy hauled her into his arms for a hug, Jamie and all.

Mitch glared at his brother's back. What was it about Jodi Hawke that attracted them both? Jodi had said Max had dropped her and that they didn't have a strong relationship, not a lot of chemistry between them, but they had gone out for a couple of months.

Then after she and Max had split he'd been feeling particularly low about his adoptive parents' bad financial situation and the bankruptcy suit that had been filed against them so he'd given Jodi a call to ask her out for a drink and a meal. One thing had led to another with Jodi that night. The chemistry between *them* had been hot, sparking and wild. He had to believe her when she said she hadn't felt anything strong for Max.

Jodi backed away from Max, the thumping of her heart unnaturally loud. She'd seen the utter disbelief in Max's eyes, quickly followed by shock when the realisation he had a nephew clanged into place. But he had hugged her as he always had, like a special friend.

Moistening her dry mouth, she filled him in a bit. 'I've been in Dunedin all the time, working for a general practice when time allows. Jamie keeps me fairly busy.'

'I imagine he does.' Max was studying Jamie carefully. Seeing the illness? Of course he was. Anyone with half a medical brain would know this wasn't a child brimming with good health.

'Jamie has cystinosis and he's been referred to Lucas Harrington. We've just come from seeing him.' Max's eyes widened, darkened as he absorbed this bit of news. She could see the thought processes going on in that bright intellect as he digested everything. Compassion clashed with surprise. Sadness nudged medical interest.

'The poor little guy,' was all he finally said, but there was a weight of concern behind each word. He really did care, really did understand what she might be going through.

'Guess you never expected to have a nephew,' she muttered.

A Maitland smile lifted the grim outline of his mouth. 'There's a good surprise in every day.'

Stunned, she could only gape at her son's uncle. No nasty words, no snips at Mitch for obviously not knowing he'd fathered a child. This Max was new to her. Swallowing the lump sliding up her throat, she managed, 'Thank you. Hopefully you'll get to see him on a day when he's got more energy and can chatter to you.'

'I look forward to it.' Max's gaze fixed on his nephew, and a flash of hunger zipped through his startled eyes. It was gone so fast she wondered if she was mistaken. Replaced by his usual professional, don't-think-you-can-touch-me demeanour. But, no, she had seen it, knew he'd be around to see Jamie some time soon. Her heart softened. Bring it on. *And sorry, Carleen Murphy, we don't need you after all. I've just touched base with the best surgeon in all respects available for Jamie.*

Jamie's eyes were closed as he sniffled against her neck. Her hands tightened around his thin body. 'I'm sorry, Max, but we have to go. Jamie's exhausted after seeing the specialist and having bloods taken.'

Mitch reached for Jamie, lifted him into his arms to relieve Jodi of her load, knowing she'd let him go now. She'd reached an understanding with Max that he hadn't been a part of but which he found he didn't mind. His brother was Jamie's best hope and so all animosity had to be set aside. He'd seen the instant Max had comprehended his role in Jamie's future.

Mitch also knew the exact moment Max fully understood the implications of Jamie's disease. There'd been a glint of compassion in the sharp glance Max had flicked him. A big question hovered behind the reality of what he'd just worked out. If Jamie needed a transplant, who was going to be the donor?

To dodge that bullet, Mitch told him, 'Jamie's to be seen in your department next week.'

Jodi murmured, 'We haven't got an appointment yet.'

Max stood absolutely still, concentrating on Jamie. Finally he shook his head and focused on Jodi. 'Bring him to see me tomorrow. Three o'clock. All right?'

And then he was gone, charging out of the canteen, a man on a mission.

'How can he know he's got a space in his schedule at that time?' Jodi stared after him.

'He'll make time. Guaranteed. But, Jodi, just because he's seeing Jamie tomorrow, it doesn't mean you can't have Carleen Murphy do the operation if that's what you want.'

She looked at him with those big imploring eyes. 'I haven't a clue what or who I want. Except…' She stopped, and shook her shoulders as though pushing aside something very difficult.

He fully understood. Especially when it came to having his brother on the case. But they had to put all grievances aside in the interest of getting the absolute best care and help for Jamie. And as much as it galled him to admit it, Max was the best transplant surgeon in the country.

Jodi leaned in against him for a brief moment. He had to bend his head to hear her say, 'No, I do know. Max has to do the transplant. If it's not asking too much of him, considering the family ties.'

That was something they'd have to wait to find out.

CHAPTER SIX

'YOU'RE NOT SAYING MUCH.' Jodi's understatement jolted him as he concentrated on the motorway traffic. 'You must be feeling annoyed that Max has found out about Jamie before you've had time to get used to the idea.'

'You could say that.' He pulled out to pass a truck and trailer unit.

'Working in the same hospital, the odds were always tipped that way.'

'We hardly ever bump into each other. Mostly keep to our own areas.' To avoid each other and the arguments that the hospital staff had come to expect as much as they did.

'What is behind all that antagonism between you two?'

He breathed deep. 'Did you know our parents died when we were six?'

'Yes, I think it was you who told me. What happened?'

He should've told her everything years ago. That's what couples did, shared their pasts as well as their futures. But they hadn't been planning on a long-term future together. At least, he hadn't. The closer Jodi had got to him the more he'd pushed her away until she'd left him and he could feel justified for his actions. Self-preservation? Or self-destruction?

'Mitch, talk to me. I need to know more about your

past. Jamie will start asking questions as he gets older.' She hiccupped and twisted her head to stare out the side window, sniffing back tears.

Mitch's heart lurched as he glanced across and saw her swallowing hard. He had to fight the urge to pull over to the side of the motorway and hug her in a vain attempt to take away her fears. She lived with Jamie's situation every minute of every day. It must hover on the periphery of her mind, suddenly blinking into full focus whenever she talked about anything but Jamie's immediate future.

But until he worked through what his role was then he had to keep his distance from her. At the moment all he could give her was some background stuff. 'Dad and Mum loved sailing, especially offshore. It was their passion.' More than their kids had been if they could go away and leave us for months at a time. 'They were on a trip to Fiji when a storm blew up. There were mayday calls for a few hours, then nothing. An air and sea search went on for days until eventually a few broken planks and a life jacket with the yacht's name stencilled on it were found a long way from their last known position. The court ruled death by drowning.'

Jodi turned to look at him through watery eyes. The hand she rested on his arm trembled. 'That's dreadful. What happened to you and Max?'

'We were separated and sent to live with different uncles, both brothers of our father. They got to choose one twin each.' A chill permeated his warm muscles, set bumps on his forearms. Like how did anyone pick between two kids?

'Twins shouldn't be separated.'

'Want to tell me something I don't know?' he snapped. 'I get that we were a handful, but we'd just lost our parents. Who wouldn't be?'

Jodi laid her hand on his arm again. 'Hey, that's shocking. Why did neither of them take both of you?'

'The uncles never got on, always competing against each other in everything.' He sighed. 'Yeah, like Max and I.' He concentrated on the car in front, keeping a perfect distance behind it. 'From what I learned over the years, Harry and Fred carried that competitive streak too far and couldn't agree about who took us so their wonderful solution was to take one each. And to hell with the consequences for us.'

It had been like losing an arm to lose his twin, only worse. And there had begun the slow build-up to the animosity that now lay between he and Max. The families had been completely different; the situations and attitudes of their adoptive parents poles apart.

'That is so cruel.'

'My adoptive family is loving and sharing. Ma and Pa were always putting their hands in their pockets for anyone to the detriment of themselves. They now live in a run-down bungalow in a bad part of town.' And refuse any offer of financial help. After all they'd done for him it saddened and maddened him. 'But despite everything they did for me, gave me, how much love I got, they weren't my parents. And my cousins were exactly that. Cousins. Not my twin brother.'

'Yes, that would suck, big time. What about Max's family?'

'He landed into a very wealthy home with people who made high demands on their adopted son. I'm not even sure they wanted children so why they adopted him is a mystery, except to get one over Harry. I lived in Ashburton; Max lived in Auckland. We never saw each other except for a couple of awkward visits.'

As a young boy, Mitch had spent years searching for

Mum and Dad, and Max, at every turn of the road, in every shop, on the bus. When he had been a teen he'd run away to Auckland in search of his brother, only to be rebuffed. He couldn't do any of that to Jamie, no matter how much he might want to be a part of the lad's life. He knew how desertion hurt deeply, irrevocably.

Mitch flicked a quick glance in the rear-view mirror at Jamie, sitting in his special seat. *My spitting image. How could I leave him?* How could he not get to know the boy?

How could he ignore the burning question he saw in Jodi's eyes every time he looked at her?

Focusing on driving so he could briefly abandon thoughts of Jodi and his son, he took the Greenlane turn-off. But the despair and worry over what to do did not back off. As if it was likely to. Somehow over the next few weeks he had to come to some decisions about Jamie.

But, wow, he was a dad to a cracker of a little guy. Despite thinking he wanted to hightail it as far away as possible, there was a spark of interest and yearning that, if he admitted to it, would never let go of its hold over him. He wasn't going to do a runner. He didn't know what he would do, how he'd make it all work, but he would do his damnedest for Jamie. And Jodi.

Could he commit to this child? If he gave Jamie his all, would it work out for them both? Doing so would keep Jodi in his life one way or another, too. Did he want that?

His gut clenched. Was that a no? Or a yes?

Why would he suddenly get a relationship right when he'd not managed one so far in thirty-six years?

Back at the motel, Jodi held the door open as Mitch carried a tired and grizzly Jamie inside to his bed and laid him down. 'Time you had a wee sleep, sport.'

'Don't want to,' said Jamie around a big yawn. 'Where's Mummy?'

'Right here, sweetheart.' Jamie had looked so right in his father's arms. Startling how similar they were, not only physically but also in their expressions. Right now Jamie wore that frustrated expression that twisted his face whenever things weren't going his way. She'd seen that expression on Mitch's face more often than she could count.

She was still getting her head round Mitch's shocking revelation about his parents' deaths and the upbringing he'd had afterwards. She couldn't begin to imagine what it must've been like to be separated from his twin. No wonder he had commitment issues. If only he'd listen if she told him she believed that having had an unusual up-bringing didn't mean he wasn't capable of being a great dad. More than many men, he'd understand how important it was to be there for his child. Unfortunately she had no chance of getting that message across.

'Mummy, where's blankie?'

She hurried to fetch the old baby blanket Jamie refused to go to bed without. 'Here it is, and I've got some medicine, too.' When Jamie opened his mouth to protest she slid the full spoon into his mouth.

'Yuck.' He shook his head in disgust.

Her heart expanded. She loved her boy so much. Today's confirmation from Lucas about the transplant had been hard to swallow, despite knowing it was coming, and yet now that she'd had time to calm down she found she was ready. Bring it on. Then they could get on with their lives.

'Who's a good boy, then?' She kissed the top of his head. Felt the heat on his skin. A flare of worry almost blinded her. She'd need the thermometer. In a moment.

First things first. 'Okay, let's take your clothes off and tuck you in all nice and snug.'

Mitch held a squirming Jamie while Jodi deftly whipped his top and trousers off. 'Want to take his temp when he's settled? I'll get your medical kit.'

'Thanks,' she muttered. So Mitch had noticed the heat on Jamie's skin too. Didn't he get the urgency of a transplant? Or was he avoiding the real issue here? He was a possible donor, a stronger candidate than anyone else. With a kidney from a compatible parent Jamie had far better odds of an excellent recovery and long-term good health. The first thing she'd done on learning Jamie had cystinosis had been to find out if she was compatible in preparation for this moment. Unfortunately, her own history of renal disease as a child had put her out of the running. And that had felt as thought she'd failed her child badly.

'Want anything else?' Mitch put her bag on the floor.

Your kidney. Closing her eyes to hide those words from him, she held her breath. Fought the impulse to grab Mitch and shake him into seeing things her way. Like that would really help. Even she knew Mitch had to make his own decisions on that score. Surely he got the urgency? Lucas did. Max did. She did.

'Jodi? You all right?'

Of course not. Who would be? Part of her knew that if she rushed him into a decision, she was less likely to get the result she wanted: help to save Jamie's life. The other part of her couldn't care less if he was hurried, she needed to know. It was too late to keep Mitch away so she'd just have to deal with the fallout of whatever he decided to do.

Sighing, she said, 'I'll be a little while here. A story always helps calm Jamie down so that he drops off to

sleep. Hopefully that'll help bring his temperature down.'
Otherwise they'd be back to the hospital before the end
of the day.

'I'll phone into work and see how they're coping with
the TV crew.' Mitch backed out of the tiny room.

'I like Mitch, Mummy.'

'Me too.' When she wasn't thinking about kidneys
and transplants. But now that she wasn't stressing about
tipping Mitch's world upside down she was starting to
see the man she'd once fallen for. Behind the concerns
and questions lurked the charming side of him. Plus the
caring, tender man. The humour hadn't come to the fore
but that was hardly surprising.

She could hear him talking on his phone, the words
indistinguishable but that deep, velvety tone sent heat
curling through her, reaching the tips of her toes, the
muscles in her neck, and everywhere in between. She
could almost feel his body under her palms, the smooth
skin, the taut muscles, the latent strength.

For the first time since she'd taken her house key off
him, memories of all the good times flooded in without
any of the baggage getting in the way. It was as though,
since arriving on Saturday, all that mess in her mind had
washed away, finally leaving her free to get to know the
father of her child all over again. Last time she'd known
Mitch as a lover, a partner. How would she know him
this time round?

*How do you want to know him? Apart from as Ja-
mie's father?*

The book in her hand shook. Moving her head left then
right, left, right, she quashed the flare of panic. No, she
wasn't going down the Mitchell path again. He might be
stepping up to the line about Jamie but she still couldn't
trust him to be there for her. Not as a husband or even

as a lover. Definitely not for ever. That would be asking too much of him. Way too much. He'd openly admitted he couldn't do it.

And since the only kind of relationship she'd ever agree to partake in involved total commitment and stability, she and Mitch were yesterday's news.

Her stomach sank. Her blood slowed. Really?

Really. There was no future for her with Mitch.

So why did her whole body feel so sluggish at that thought?

'Jodi,' Mitch whispered from the doorway. 'Jamie's sound asleep.'

'Oh. That was quick, but I guess he's exhausted after all the drama of meeting Dr Harrington.' At least Mitch didn't know where she'd been in her head. Tucking the cover under Jamie's chin, she tiptoed out and carefully closed the door.

Mitch stood in the middle of the main room. His size made the walls shrink in on her. His gentle, caring gaze made her heart trip and her breathing falter.

This was a Mitch she'd not met before.

This was a Mitch she had to be very wary of if she wanted to remain untouched by him. She needed to keep her head straight and not give in to any fantasies about falling in love with him again.

Her heart stuttered in defiance. Why not? He's the only man who'd ever made her pulse beat as though she'd run a marathon, made her body feel starved until he touched her.

She gasped. What's happening here? She'd tracked down Mitch for Jamie's sake, not because she needed him. Not because she'd never forgotten him. Or because she'd never stopped wishing he was still a part of her life. Within two days all those pent-up emotions and feelings that only Mitch could evoke were roaring around her head, through her body, centring at her core. Making her want to drag him off to bed and have her wicked way with what she knew that superb suit covered.

Heat swamped her face and she turned aside before Mitch could read the emotions that surely must be spreading through her eyes, over her cheeks and curving her lips into a sultry smile.

'Want a coffee? I have to warn you, I've only got instant.' Not that she wanted another hot drink but she did want to keep her hands busy and away from Mitch.

'No, thanks.' Mitch watched Jodi's lips press together with worry as she dropped onto the arm of one of the two chairs in the room.

He needed her, wanted her, had the urge to haul her into his arms and hug her until she finally relaxed and smiled that beautiful, gut-wrenching smile he always used to look for at the end of the shift when he finally walked through the front door of the flat he'd shared with her.

It might be a dumb move but he put all his reservations aside and moved to lift her up and wrap his arms around her thin frame. Damn, but she needed feeding up. 'Hey, let me hold you for a moment. You look shattered.' Pulling her against his chest, he tucked her head neatly under his chin and held her. Right where she belonged: in his arms.

Until this moment he hadn't realised he'd missed her so much. Hadn't understood that he was only half a man without Jodi in his life. Until now he'd believed he'd had everything he needed. That there was no room in his life, his heart to fit someone close. Someone special. Jodi. He'd known he'd screwed up. But now it was as though someone had taken a bat and banged him over the head until he got the message. Jodi was the only woman for him.

He'd neglected her back then. Big time. He'd let her kick him out, taking the easy option, thanking his lucky stars that he'd escaped unscathed. But he'd been lying to himself. Pleased that he'd proved she wasn't a stayer.

Unscathed? Yeah, right. As if. If that cold, lonely town house of his, the one-night stands that he never took back to his place, no one to share a birthday or Christmas with, was what he really wanted, then fine. Go for it. Enjoy it. Make the most of what he had. If that was his definition of unscathed and happy then he was a sad puppy.

He'd definitely been lying to himself. All along. Worse—he'd always known he had been.

So what now? Declare his feelings? Tell Jodi he actually cared for her, about her? That he wanted to be right at her side over the next months as Jamie battled for his life? That he wanted to be there for her beyond that? His stomach crunched, his heart dived for cover. Go ahead, tell her all that and then stand back while she laughs herself sick.

Jodi was not stupid. She would not believe a word of it. And who could blame her? Certainly not him.

So what now? Slowly, slowly, sort one problem out at a time. Over her head he stared at the crappy motel room, the marked walls, the grimy windows and shabby furniture. Unwinding his arms from around her body, he stepped back. 'Have you done anything about finding a flat to move in to?'

She tensed. 'I've hardly had time.'

'Good.' He reached into his back pocket. 'The key to my front door. It's only a small place, and we'll be a bit squeezed, but pack your bags and move in. Today.' When her mouth fell open, he couldn't help adding, 'For as long as you need somewhere to live in Auckland.'

It felt great to surprise her in a good way. He caught up one of her hands, wrapped her fingers around the key. 'You can't stay in this motel. It's awful. Not good for a sick child. Not exactly cheerful for you either. Oh, and here's another key. Get rid of that heap on wheels you've rented. From now on, my vehicle is yours.'

Those brown pools fixed on him, filled with amazement and gratitude. 'Are you sure? There are three of us. Mum's not going back down south until Friday.'

'No problem. I've got two spare bedrooms. Anyway, I'm not there very often.'

'To sleep and shower, according to your cleaning lady.' Jodi looked guilty. 'I met her on Saturday when I went looking for you.'

'I wondered why you turned up at the hospital in the evening. Get tired of waiting for me to come home?' Just like old times. He swallowed the bile rising in his throat. Hell, home wasn't his favourite place. Not a lot going on there.

'How will you get around if I've got your car?'

'I'll grab a taxi. Or give you a call.' It was less than two months until he left for Sydney. Oh, hell. Sydney and the job of a lifetime. So much to sort out. So much to consider. Too much to think about. Slowly, slowly, one small thing at a time. 'I'll go and talk to the motelier while you pack up.'

Jodi watched Mitch stride across to the motel office, his shoulders back and his chin forward. So full of confidence. His way was the right way. No doubts at all. 'You still don't ask what I'd like to do.' Her mouth curved upward. 'You just tell me.' Funny how today she couldn't care less when in the past she'd have refused just to spite him.

'I take it you're not talking to yourself.' Mum spoke from the doorway, laden down with full recycle grocery bags. 'And as I see Mitch disappearing into the poky space the owners of this dump call an office, you must be berating him.'

Jodi opened her hand to show the keys. 'We're moving into his house as soon as Jamie wakes up. And the other key is for that fancy four-wheel drive parked outside.'

Mum dumped her shopping on the bench and turned to study her daughter in a disconcerting, this-is-your-mother-talking kind of way. 'Good. He's come through for you both. Always thought he would if he was pushed hard enough. And there's nothing harder than being confronted with the son he didn't know he had. Good man.'

So much for wondering if Mum would move into Mitch's place with them. She'd probably have come up with the idea herself in a day or two if Mitch hadn't beaten her to it. 'Mum, you've never liked the guy. Remember all the things you used to warn me about? Newsflash—most of them came true.'

'Selective memory, my girl. I also used to say Mitch Maitland would make a fabulous husband if he ever got over his past. It can't have been easy, growing up without his parents there and never seeing his twin brother. He's done amazingly well considering the circumstances.'

Jodi gaped. 'You knew all that? How? He never even told me.'

'You didn't think I wouldn't check up on my grandson's parentage, did you? I always thought there was more to Mitch and Max than was obvious. They might be charmers who're used to getting what they want from everyone they cross paths with but essentially they're good men.' Mum winced. 'I should've told you what I learned but I figured you had enough on your plate with Jamie's illness. How did the hospital consultation go, by the way?'

Stunned at her mother's revelation, Jodi took a moment to answer the sudden question about something totally different, and then she didn't have to.

Mitch answered for her as he came inside. 'Lucas Harrington is excellent and I have every confidence in him. But even though I knew what was coming, he still managed to shock me to the core. I presume Jodi's heard what he had to say before, but hearing it again rattled her too.'

'It's so different when it's my...' Jodi swallowed. 'When he's talking about our child. It doesn't matter how many discussions I've had with Jamie's specialists, the details still scare me sick.'

Mitch's eyebrows rose endearingly. 'Yes, that must be it. Not any old patient but our son.'

Mum looked from Mitch to her and back again. 'So, is this Dr Harrington putting Jamie on the transplant waiting list?'

'Yes. We've got an appointment with the transplant team tomorrow afternoon.' Mitch moved closer to Jodi and casually dropped an arm over her shoulders.

His warmth and strength immediately filtered through to her, touching that chilly place where all things to do with Jamie's health hid. She snuggled even nearer. Drawing a breath, she told her mother, 'Max is arranging the appointment. We bumped into him at the canteen and the moment he heard about Jamie's problem he gave us a time to go and see him.'

Mum didn't even blink. 'I'm glad. We want the absolute best treatment for Jamie, and in Max's hands he'll get it.'

So she'd known Max worked at Auckland General too. Just how much had Mum found out about the Maitland twins in that research she'd done? And why hadn't she talked about this before now? Could've saved some worry about how to tell Mum that both brothers were here and that there was every possibility they'd both have something to do with Jamie's care.

Mitch shook his head. 'We're waiting to see how tomorrow's meeting goes before deciding that.'

We are? She wasn't so sure, though she was still struggling with Max being a part of this. In the meantime she'd back Mitch even if he was definitely against his brother doing the transplant if at all possible. Presumably they had time to think it all through, that a kidney wouldn't become available in the next day or two. 'Yes, that's right.'

Mum said nothing, just rolled her shoulders and looked away, lost in her own thoughts.

Mitch squeezed Jodi's shoulder. 'I've checked you out of here as from whenever you're ready to go. You've got all afternoon if you need it.'

'Jamie will sleep for a couple of hours, then there's nothing else to keep us here.' From under his arm she turned to look at him. 'Don't you need to go to work? That TV crew could be having a wonderful time without you there to restrain them.' It was one thing for him to accompany them to see Lucas but quite another to hang around all morning with her.

'Aaron will be more of a ball and chain with them than I'd ever be.' With one finger he lifted her hair out of her eyes. The steady blue gaze he fixed on her sent electricity zipping along her veins, reminding her of how well they'd played together. Unfortunately his voice was solemn, reminding her how out of kilter they were now. 'But I do have to put in an appearance. I can't ask Aaron to work my whole shift and then do his tonight.'

Plastering on a smile, Jodi gave him the answer he would want. 'Then go. We've only got three bags. I can get us packed and moved to your place easy as.' And she needed space to sort through these weird feelings ambushing her every time Mitch touched her.

Not to mention how, as much as she wanted Mitch in on everything to do with Jamie's treatment, she was so used to going it alone that it felt a little stifling having him just hanging around now that they were back at the motel.

'There's a GPS in my vehicle.'

'Handy.' If she knew how to use one. 'Can you warn Claire she's going to be overrun with Hawkes?'

'Done already. She's making beds as we speak.' Mitch didn't move, didn't shift that penetrating gaze.

What did he see? She'd changed in the time they'd been apart. Having a sick child did that. Blast it, she didn't even take care of her appearance anymore. Her smile deepened. She'd set a new fashion trend—grunge. Oh, but that had already been done; she was just running behind the times.

Mitch leaned forward and placed the lightest of light kisses on her cheek. So gentle that it brought tears to her eyes. That kiss spoke of affection, care and support. It told her she still held a place in his heart, even if only that of the mother of his son.

And then it hit her. Pine with a hint of spice. His aftershave. The one she used to buy him. He hadn't been wearing it over the weekend—she'd definitely have noticed. But now he was. So there was more to his kiss than affection. But just how much more? What was he telling her? She was afraid to find out. Didn't want to go there.

To break her heart over him once had been bad enough; to do it again would be stupid. And she was a lot of things, but stupid wasn't one of them.

CHAPTER SEVEN

MITCH PAID THE taxi driver and shoved open the door. Home at last. The television crew had trailed after him all afternoon and right into the evening. Their endless questions had at times annoyed him but in the interests of getting a real and true picture of how an emergency department worked he'd sucked it up and done his best to be helpful.

All the while wanting to go home and check out Jamie. To make sure that temperature had gone down. Check Jodi was okay after their eventful morning.

His legs dragged with weariness as he headed up the path, but his heart lifted at the welcoming scene. Lights were on behind the drawn curtains, the light on over the front door. The first time that had happened since he'd moved in last year.

The large bag with the toyshop logo swung back and forth from his fingers. He'd snatched a quick break and gone out to the toyshop next to the hospital, strategically placed for softies like him.

Humming tunelessly, Mitch pushed the door open. Swallowed hard as the words, 'Hi, honey, I'm home' nearly spilled off his tongue. Repeating something that had amused her three years ago would only make her think he was deliberately trying to use the past to win her over. Which he was—kind of. Cramming his size-ten foot into his mouth to shut him up might be a better option. Jodi would probably brain him with a pan if those words reached her pretty ears.

Another memory assailed him. Where were the earrings? He hadn't seen Jodi wearing any since she'd appeared in his office on Saturday. She was queen of earrings and bracelets. Not a bracelet in sight either. The woman had jewellery boxes full of them. Surely she still did? Had they gone into storage along with all those swanky clothes she loved to wear? Maybe she'd given them to the op shop. But why? The woman he knew couldn't have changed that much. Had she? Nah, he kept seeing hints of the old Jodi. Surely beneath that worry and fear for her boy lay the happy, jokey Jodi who loved to dance and tease.

'Hey there, you obviously got busy.' Jodi didn't add *considering it's after nine*, but he heard the words anyway and bit down on a retort. They hadn't moved along that far in their relationship. Yet. If ever. That kiss at the park hadn't changed a thing.

Yeah, it had. He'd rediscovered his Jodi, remember? Yeah. That had something going for it.

Striding towards the kitchen where she stood in the doorway, he told her, 'It wasn't horrendously busy with patients but the TV crew made up for that. Then I told Aaron to stay away until nine to make up for filling in for me this morning.'

Her cheeks reddened deliciously. 'Oops. I spoke without thinking.'

'An old habit?' he snipped. Then, 'Sorry. Uncalled for. It's odd finding people in my house at the end of a day at work.' He looked around. 'I take it Jamie's asleep?' He put down the bag he held, ignoring a flare of disappointment. Of course the lad would be in bed at this hour.

'Out for the count despite his excitement about staying in Mitch's house.' Her smile was shy. The lookalike Jodi had returned. The old Jodi had never done shy.

Sniffing the air appreciatively, he said, 'Something smells wonderful.' How easy it would be to get used to this. Even if it meant coming home earlier? 'Never thought to tell you I hardly ever eat here and that the cupboards were bare.'

Jodi stepped backwards into the kitchen, a gorgeous smile lightening up her face. 'All taken care of. Mum went shopping, and I put together a lasagne and salad. Hope that's okay?'

'Okay? You have no idea.' Anything edible would be okay. Lasagne and salad made his mouth water. 'Have you eaten?'

'Thought I'd wait for you. Mum had hers and has taken herself off to her room to start reading her financial reports.'

Unless Alison was a ditz she must've made a fortune over the years with all the financial shuffling she'd done, and she was no ditz. Yet there was no sign of wealth. That motel and the rental car he'd dropped off on the way to work indicated a distinct lack of funds. Puzzling, but not important. What was important was spending the rest of the evening with Jodi. 'Do you want a glass of wine before we eat? That is one thing I do have plenty of.'

'I opened a bottle of Cabernet Merlot to breathe. Hope you don't mind?' Jodi handed him the bottle and held out two glasses to be filled.

'You certainly knew which one to pick.' He grinned at the top choice she'd made.

'That's quite a collection in your cellar. Since when did you become a wine buff?'

'I've always enjoyed a good wine, but until I came to Auckland I'd never really done much about it. Besides, med students drink beer. These days, when I take a weekend off, I like to get out of town and away from the possibility of being called into work, so I've started visiting the North Island wine-growing regions. Funny how those bottles seem to find their way into my car with no trouble at all.'

'Right. You open the door and shoo them in. I can see it now.' Laughter tinkled in the kitchen air.

Mitch felt his eyes widening as he realised that was the first time he'd heard Jodi laugh these past days. 'You should do that more often.'

'Do what?'

'Laugh.' He took a gulp of wine. 'You used to always be laughing about something.' And when her face dropped he hastily added, 'I know you haven't had a lot to laugh about. Believe me, I get it. But hearing that just then brought back some wonderful memories.' Another swallow of wine. 'We weren't all bad together. There were plenty of fun times too.' Mostly in the sack. Because there hadn't been time for much else. What an idiot. He'd gone and made things worse, just when they'd started getting along a wee bit better.

Any minute now she'd throw her wine in his face, tell him he was a selfish pig and that she was moving back to that rank motel. He waited and watched.

Jodi blinked. Stared at him. Then her mouth lifted into a wide, beautiful smile. That gut-wrenching smile all his dreams and memories were made of. 'Thank you for reminding me. Sometimes all I've been able to think about is the wrong memories.' The colour heightened delightfully in her cheeks, over her throat. The tip of her tongue grazed her lips. 'I've been having some memories of my own since yesterday.'

Since he'd kissed her? 'Really?'

'Some of the good ones.' The heat in her eyes scorched him, told him exactly which good times she recollected.

Memories skittered across his skin bringing back exquisite sensations of his body sliding over hers, his hands recalled touching the dip of her waist and that soft place on her inner thighs, and cupping those curvy buttocks. His tongue knew the taste of her. Below his belt his maleness definitely remembered the very centre of her femininity. It sprang up, hard and hopeful. 'Down boy,' he growled under his breath. Wrong place. Wrong time. Bad, bad—good.

He lifted one foot to close the gap between them. Panic flared in those coffee-*au-lait* eyes. Her sweet mouth flattened. A slight jerk of her head negated his move. His shoe slapped on the tile floor. Bad, bad, bad.

Spinning around, Jodi was suddenly very busy serving up dinner. The dinner he no longer wanted. But what he wanted he couldn't have. Not now. Not ever.

Over lunch in his office the next day Mitch spent a lot of time answering the TV documentary director's questions methodically, keeping the medical content to a minimum without actually dumbing everything down too much. Now he needed to do some real work. He pushed his empty coffee cup aside. 'If that's all for the moment?'

Carl stood up, smiling good-naturedly. 'Sure. I know you're busy and I'm a pain in the butt.'

Mitch grinned back. 'We understand each other. So how do you think your documentary is working out? Are you getting some good footage of the patients and what we deal with?'

'Absolutely. Your staff have been extremely accommodating to my crews.'

'Right down to getting their hair done and wearing more make-up in a couple of days than any of them normally use in a year.'

Carl chuckled. 'I'm used to that. The moment the word "camera" is uttered, out comes the lipstick and hairbrush.' His face grew more serious. 'We're getting good footage but what I want now is a human-interest story that can run through the whole doco, tie it all together.'

Mitch winced. They'd discussed this prior to the crews starting in the department and he wasn't so sure that he liked the idea. 'Have you given consideration to how patients might come to regret it if they say yes while they're dealing with pain and serious injuries?'

'They'd have the opportunity to change their minds later. Whether that person is the patient or the patient's parent or caregiver,' Carl reminded him.

'So you don't think any of the patients you've filmed so far suit your criteria?'

'Mitch.' Samantha flew in the door. 'Mitch, you've got to come now. The ambulance has brought in a little boy with acute renal failure.'

Mitch's heart stopped. 'Do we have a name for this child?' The question squeezed through his clenched teeth.

'Jamie Hawke.' Samantha's eyes were huge in her face, and there was a hint of something awfully like excitement as she added, 'Jamie Maitland Hawke.'

Mitch's chair flew backwards. Snatching up his phone, he scanned the messages as he raced for the cubicles. Nothing. Jodi hadn't phoned or texted. Why not? If he was picking up the reins of fatherhood then she had to include him in everything happening to Jamie. 'Where is he?' he demanded.

'Cubicle four.' Samantha ran alongside him. 'Is Jamie a relation of yours?'

'Yes.' More information than she needed to know.

'I'll tell the cameraman to head your way.' Carl was with him too.

'No. You. Won't.' He snarled. 'Stay away from this patient.'

'I didn't think Max had any kids.' Samantha had skin thicker than a rhinoceros's.

'He doesn't.' Oh, hell. Mitch cursed under his gasping breath. Now the whole department, no, the whole hospital would know he had a son by dinnertime. Not that he wanted to hide the fact, but he wasn't ready to share any of Jamie's story with *everybody.*

At cubicle four he jerked the curtain open and strode in. And stopped. Jamie was attached to more cables and tubes than a cat had lives. 'Jamie.' His gut clenched, threatened to throw his lunch back at him. Closing his eyes, he willed his belly to behave.

'Mitch?' Jodi's hand gripped his. 'We need Lucas here now. I told the nurse that but he insisted we wait until you arrived.'

Mitch blinked, stared down into the terrified face of his boy's mother. 'I'll call him. Don't you worry about that. Where is the PRF?' He snapped his fingers at Chas.

The head nurse on day shift pressed the patient report form from the ambulance into his hand. 'Severe vomiting and bloody stools. High temperature.' Chas continued talking, filling in all the details he'd gleaned from the ambulance crew.

Mitch was grateful to him. There was no way he could see the obs on the page in front of him for the tears blurring his eyes. As he listened he stepped up to the bed, ran a finger lightly down Jamie's arm, careful to avoid all the gear attached to him. 'Hey, sport,' he whispered around the lump cutting off the air to his lungs.

Chas finished the report and told Samantha, 'Get the phone and the phone number list for Mitch.'

Jodi muttered, 'Thanks, Chas.' Then her fingers squeezed Mitch's hand again. He could feel her fear through her grip. 'It happened so fast. He was a bit grizzly and his temperature had crept up some more so I put him down for a nap. When I went in to check up on him he was vomiting. I called the ambulance to save time. The way I was panicking I'd have got lost for sure.'

'We'll get Lucas down here ASAP.' He wrapped an arm around her shaking shoulders, drew her close. 'Where's that damned phone?' he yelled through the gap in the curtains. Carl stood to one side observing everything, his cameraman filming from an unobtrusive distance. Doing exactly what he'd been asked to do when any urgent cases presented. 'Not this patient, Carl.' And when Carl made to reply he held a hand up. 'Not open to negotiation.' His son was not going to make headlines on national television.

Then Samantha handed him the phone, her demeanour now serious and concerned. Had one of the nurses put her in her place? 'Extension 324 for Mr Harrington.'

Punching in the numbers, Mitch watched over his son, despair gnawing at him. The little lad hadn't moved in the minutes he'd been with him. At least he couldn't see the pain and fright behind those fragile eyelids. But he knew it was there. He'd give anything to make it all go away for Jamie.

Even your kidney?

Even my kidney.

Wouldn't Carl love that story for his show?

Mitch shuddered. He could see the show headlines already. 'Carl, go away.'

'How's Jamie doing?' Mitch's hand cupped Jodi's shoulder, his fingers firm yet calming, strong yet tender.

She hadn't heard him enter the room but, then, she hadn't heard all the hospital noises going on around her either. Jamie was her only concern, her only focus. Jodi leaned her head sideways so her cheek touched his fingers, gathering strength from him. 'Lucas just called by and gave him a top-up of antibiotics and a whole heap of other things.'

'I passed him on my way here. He's going to talk to Max, who's rescheduling our appointment with the transplant team.' Mitch squeezed her shoulder and dropped a kiss on her head.

That felt so right—as though they were on the same page. 'Everyone's being awesome.'

'We figured you've had enough drama for one day, and another twenty-four hours isn't going to bring the transplant surgery any closer.'

'I guess you're right, though I'd feel a little bit better knowing we had everything under way.' Her bottom lip trembled when she looked at him. 'But you're right. Tomorrow will do fine.'

'It's going to mean more tests, another round of poking and prodding for the little guy.' His voice was so sad, hurting even.

Jodi reached up, laid her hand over his. She didn't feel any better. In fact, she felt like crap. 'I'm glad you're here for him. Sorry to dump you in at the deep end, though. If it helps, I wish I could turn back the clock to when I learned I was pregnant. You'd be the first to know.' Her sigh was sad. 'But I guess that doesn't make you any less angry at me.'

Mitch lifted her chin with his finger. 'Anger hasn't come into it. Disappointment, yes. And sadness. But there's also guilt. If I'd come knocking on your door and explained a few things, we might've worked something out so that you'd have trusted me to be a good dad. Even if we hadn't got back together.'

His tone was so sad she had to wonder if that's what he might've wanted after all. Them together, permanently. No way. Mitch was always too busy, too tied up in his own world to make that work. Or was she being unfair? Using that to justify her own actions? Ironic when now she'd change everything if she had the chance. 'Only one way to go now. Forward.'

He didn't say anything for a while. Nothing to say, she supposed. They were parents grappling with a huge problem and finding their way back to each other with all that was going on wouldn't exactly be easy.

Finally Mitch asked, 'How's the dialysis going?'

'Doing its job, thank goodness. With the cycler working overnight, hopefully Jamie will be feeling a lot better in the morning. But I never get used to this,' she murmured. 'No matter how many times we end up in hospital, every visit is as frightening as the first one.' With her other hand she stroked Jamie's arm. 'Even with all the swelling he looks so small in this enormous bed. So frail. So darned ill.' Tears pricked the backs of her eyelids and she squeezed tight to prevent them spilling down her face. She had to be strong for Jamie. It would never do for him to wake up and see her crying.

Mitch must have sensed her fragility because he wrapped his arms around her from behind, his hands meeting beneath her breasts and pulling her back against his waist. 'Shh, you're doing fine. Just fine. How the hell you've managed to stay sane this long I can't begin to understand. I'm new to this and I'm already feeling wrecked.'

Sniff, sniff. Winding her hands around his, she told him, 'Not a lot of choice. One of those situations that when faced with you get on and do what has to be done. And that's another thing. There's not much I can do for Jamie. As a doctor or as a mum. Some days I feel so utterly helpless.'

His chin dropped onto the top of her head. 'Being a mum, being with him all the time, is the most important role. I'd bet anything that if you could ask Jamie he'd agree with me. Nothing, nobody, is as important to have around as your mum. Especially when life is going horribly pear-shaped. Believe me, I know.'

Was this the little boy whose mother died speaking here? 'Thank you. I really needed to hear that.' How had Mitch survived that shock and hurt? Even if his adoptive family had been kind and loving he'd have always carried a deep sense of loss. Even more because his twin had been taken away as well. Without thinking, she lifted his hand and kissed his palm.

He asked, 'Want a break? Take a shower? Grab something to eat? I'll sit with Jamie. The staff will page me if anything urgent comes up in ED.'

Shaking her head, 'No, I don't want to leave him in case he wakes. He'll panic if I'm not here. I'm sorry, Mitch, but he's not used to you yet. Not enough to be happy I'm not in sight when he wakes in a strange place anyway. Not that hospital is strange to him, I suppose.'

'It's okay, I get it.'

Leaning over the bed, she tucked Jamie's blankie closer to his pillow so he could see it when he woke up.

'Mind you, when he sees that teddy bear you brought him he might be more than happy for you to be with him.' A tired chuckle escaped her. 'I don't suppose they had any small bears in that shop?'

'Define small.'

'Something not as tall as Jamie.'

'Nope, not a one. Not a good-looking one, anyway.' Mitch was studying her with a serious gleam in his eye.

'What?'

'You mightn't want to leave Jamie but you do need to eat. I'll go and get you something, plus some decent coffee.'

'Thanks, but I'm not hungry.'

'Jodi, you've got to eat. Look at you, fading away to nothing. I'm guessing that's because your appetite goes every time Jamie has another serious bout of his cystinosis.'

'I needed to lose weight.' As much as ten kilos? None of her gorgeous clothes fit anymore. Not that she ever went out anywhere to wear them. At work she tended to stick to simple trousers and blouses. No point tarting herself up to be coughed or puked on.

'I'm going to the café. Any preferences?' When she shook her head he leaned closer. 'I liked you exactly as you were. Your figure was fabulous. Not that it's as important as what's on the inside. And that's fabulous too.'

By the time she'd dredged up a fitting retort Mitch had gone, leaving her to wonder what the hell was going on here. He was being so helpful and caring, supportive and bossy. Needed fattening up indeed.

Oh, okay. Fabulous on the inside. Wow. She could take as many compliments as Mitch wanted to dish out, but where did they come from? Why now and not when they had been together? Hugging herself, she enjoyed the warmth seeping through her.

Then her stomach rumbled and she had to concede another point. 'I get the picture. I'm apparently hungry. I'll do my best to eat whatever Mitch brings me.'

Mitch stood in the doorway to Jamie's room with a pizza box in one hand and a soda can in the other. He was late back, having been called to the ED just as he'd stepped outside the hospital. A teenager who'd been huffing gas. God damn it, when were these kids going to learn they couldn't abuse their bodies and keep getting away with it? It had been touch and go but, fingers crossed and with a lot of intensive medical care, the girl would make it through the night.

He studied Jodi. Quiet, slumped and yet very busy. Watching over her boy. Watching every breath he took. Observing the tubes putting goodies into him. Keeping a wary eye on the cycler that was emptying Jamie's abdomen of wastes, chemicals and extra water. Hopefully reducing the fluid retention that made Jamie so bloated.

'Ah, Jodi, sweetheart, you're awesome.' The words were so quiet even he didn't really hear them. Which was just as well. He did not want to see the disbelief in her eyes if she'd overheard.

He'd swear that she'd breathe for Jamie if she could. She'd certainly stick the needles and tubes into her body if that would save Jamie any discomfort. A true mother. An extraordinary woman. But, then, he'd always known that. That's why he'd been attracted to her.

Her looks and figure had drawn him first, but it had been her sense of joy—now missing—in everything, her love of life, the kindnesses and selflessness, her inner strength that had had him going back to her again and again for just one more date. That was what had stopped him leaving her after only a few weeks, as he'd done with all the other women he'd known. Before and after Jodi.

Jodi had set a benchmark that he'd not found since in any woman he'd taken out. Not that he'd been actively looking. Too busy avoiding staying around too long. Whereas Jodi had come from behind and slapped him on the head while he hadn't been looking. Unfortunately he'd probably made the biggest mistake of his sorry life when he'd let her get away. He hadn't recognised the emotion he'd felt for her that had churned through him as love. Plain and simple. Love. Complex and distracting. He hadn't wanted to be distracted from his game plan of getting the top job in his chosen path. A little longer and he'd have had it all.

Talk about dumb. And now it was too late. He couldn't make up for not being there during Jamie's illnesses. Even if Jodi hadn't given him the opportunity, he had to take the blame. It had been his ho-hum attitude to their relationship that had had her packing his bags. His lack of commitment that had prevented her telling him he was a father. Because, to her, he was as irresponsible as her own father. How stupid could a bloke be?

'Is that real coffee I can smell?' the woman who had his hormones and emotions on a roller-coaster ride asked.

'Sure is. And a pepperoni and triple-cheese pizza.'

'Very tempting.' Her eyes gleamed with gratitude, making him feel pleased he'd done something right for her. And then her tongue licked the corner of her mouth and he tripped over his own feet as he crossed to the bed.

More than his feet were having difficulty ignoring that gesture. South of his belt his maleness sat up, so aware of her it frightened him. Definitely not the time or place to be thinking anything sexual. That tongue flick must've been a subconscious move on Jodi's part, surely? She didn't look at all interested in anything but her coffee.

Guess it was good one of them had their priorities right.

'Hey, hope I'm not intruding?' Carl hovered in the door. 'Came to see how the little guy was doing.'

'You didn't bring the film crew with you?'

'Everyone's taking a break.' Carl gave an easy smile. 'Even we're learning to grab five when it's quiet.'

Jodi was watching Carl, caution tightening her mouth. 'You're one of the TV crew members? Is that why you were in the ED?'

Mitch made the introduction. 'Carl is in charge of the crews and does all the planning required.'

Carl stretched a hand in Jodi's direction. 'You're Mitch's wife?' In the silence that followed only Carl looked totally comfortable. 'Partner?'

Jodi shrugged and sucked a breath through her teeth. 'We're Jamie's parents.'

Mitch gave the guy credit for not making any ridiculously obvious comments, instead shifting along the bed to look down at Jamie. 'How's he doing? Better than when you first brought him in, I hope.'

Jodi answered. 'Dialysis makes him more comfortable but the catheter irritates his tummy, which he hates. He's always weary. His day is filled with short naps.'

'What's the treatment for—what was it—cystinosis?'

'Yes, cystinosis. Jamie gets regular dialysis to remove all the poisons and waste that kidneys do in healthy people. Long term?' Jodi stared at Carl, drilling him with her dark eyes. 'We wait for a kidney to become available.'

'That's all we can do,' Mitch added, to forestall the questions that smart brain opposite him was coming up with. Give Carl time and he'd know all there was to know about Jamie's condition and the odds on a kidney becoming available. He'd research everything and learn that the head of the department he was filming in had to be the most likely donor. Then try keeping the guy and his cameras away. 'Impossible situation,' he muttered.

'I can see that it is.' Carl looked pensive, craftily hiding the questions that had to be popping up.

'So you can see why I'm not interested in you filming Jamie. This is too traumatic for him as it is.'

'What's this?' Jodi reared up. 'What are you talking about? Filming?'

Carl spoke quickly. 'Wait. Don't jump to conclusions. Mitch knows I'm looking for one case coming from his department that I can follow through on. You know, the patient moving from the emergency department to a ward and then the treatment they receive, whether it's surgery or cardiac intervention. Whatever.'

'And you think Jamie is the perfect choice?' Jodi whispered.

'Truthfully? Yes, I do. It is a great human-interest story. But…' he held his hand up as Jodi's mouth opened '…I have a daughter about Jamie's age and I doubt I'd want me poking a camera in her face to make a documentary. So, good television or not, I'm not going to ask you to allow my crews near your son. Unless you change your mind, of course.' He turned to Mitch.

'Not likely.'

'It could help with making people aware of donating their organs,' Jodi commented thoughtfully, chewing at her fingernail and watching Carl with a more cautious gaze now.

Shocked, Mitch could only stare at her.

'Exactly.' Carl studied her back, trying to fathom where she was going with this.

Jodi looked too damned thoughtful. 'A lot of people indicate they want to be a donor, go to the trouble of registering the fact on their motor-vehicle licence, only to have family members refuse to follow their loved one's wishes.'

Carl sat on the end of Jamie's bed, careful not to disturb the sleeping boy. 'Not many people realise that small children are the recipients of a lot of these organs. I believe if we can show that then the donor numbers will rise significantly.'

Forget this guy going to do his research. He'd already done it. 'Leave it, Carl. Jodi has a lot to deal with already, without having cameras in her face.'

'To a certain extent I agree. But I'll leave it with you.' Carl nodded at the box Mitch had forgotten was in his hands. 'That pizza's getting cold.'

What he hadn't forgotten was the result of the blood-group test he'd had done that afternoon on the spur of the moment. Just in case he did decide to look more seriously at donating a kidney. It would be silly to put himself through making that decision only to find his blood group was no use to Jamie.

The result had told him he was Type O. Perfectly compatible with Jamie's Type A.

But it was too soon to tell Jodi. No point in getting her hopes up until he knew for sure what he would do.

CHAPTER EIGHT

JODI COULD FEEL Mitch beside her, fuming at his brother as the whole transplant team crowded around Jamie's bed, talking and reading notes. Overkill, surely? She'd have been happy to talk to Carleen Murphy. Or Max. Just not the whole bang lot of them. Even Lucas had turned up. They had Jamie's interests at heart but didn't they understand how terrifying this was for the little guy?

And while Mitch was fuming, Jamie was fretting. The corner of his blankie was stuffed in his mouth, slobber soaking the thick fabric. Tears streaked his pale cheeks. The shock of his admittance and then being put on dialysis had taken its toll on her boy. Leaning closer, she ran her hand over his head, and gave him a wink. 'Hey, Jamie, love, Mummy's here.'

'Want to go home,' he hiccupped, his eyes wide as he tried to beguile her into taking him out of there, away to where it was quiet and nice, not noisy and scary, not hurting.

'Not yet, sweetheart. These people are going to make you better.'

When the bewilderment filtered into his eyes she felt bad. Lying to her son had become a habit. Even Jamie understood that these people might not make him better. No other doctor had fixed him. When kids were seriously ill they seemed to mature so much in some aspects of their lives. There was no fooling Jamie that his body was improving.

But she could do something for him. Straightening her spine, she took her despair out on those who might understand it. 'If you're all going to hang around discussing Jamie's problems then you can at least sit down. You're huge from his perspective. Intimidating and scary,' she snapped.

'There aren't enough chairs to go round,' someone, she didn't know who, muttered.

He could go. She didn't need anyone on the team who couldn't see this from Jamie's point of view. 'Find some or leave.'

One of Max's eyebrows rose disconcertingly but there was a hint of approval in his gaze before he turned to a hovering nurse and flashed his charming smile. 'Find some more chairs, please, Charmaine.'

The nurse smiled ever so sweetly before dashing off to do Max's biding.

Ignoring the byplay, Jodi sighed. Was she overreacting? Damn right she was. This was her baby. And as if that wasn't bad enough, Mitch had been fuming quietly from the moment Max had walked in and said something to him. What, she didn't have a clue. When would these two get over their differences and act like family? They didn't have anyone else. Surely they needed each other?

Her eyes returned to Jamie. He was their family too, damn it. Mitch's son. Max's nephew. Family. Like it or not. 'Max…' She curled her forefinger to beckon him close. Thankfully he joined her and Mitch, otherwise she didn't know what she'd have done. Probably shouted at them, turning the ward into a zoo.

Keeping her voice low, she said, 'This is not an ideal

situation for you both, but I don't care. This is about Jamie
and not whatever you two have going on.' She stabbed
the air between them and growled, 'Bury it while we
make Jamie better. Nothing else matters at all.' Her finger hit Mitch's chest. 'Your son.' Then Max's arm. 'Your
nephew.'

Sinking back into her chair, she returned her focus to
Jamie, feeling uncomfortable. Had that been wise? Had
she gone too far? Probably. But she was allowed to. She
was a mother.

Mitch studied Max, trying to really see him, to see past
all their angst. This was the man Mitch always wanted
to outdo, and yet now he was about to rely on him for
the biggest dilemma of his life. Jodi was right. He knew
that. But there was too much history between him and
his brother just to bury it in an instant. He'd spent his life
being told that if he wanted to get ahead he had to do better than Max. And because the relatives that had adopted
him were dirt poor he'd felt justified in proving to them
they were right to believe in him and that he didn't need
the wealth Max had lucked into.

What if Max had been fed the same line of rubbish
about him? It was something to consider. But not now.
Today was about Jamie, not them. If he couldn't at least
talk to Max for the duration of Jamie's treatment then he
had to leave now, head to Sydney on the next flight and
never look back.

Sucking in his gut, he met Max's eyes and stuck out
his hand. 'Let's put aside everything other than Jamie for
as long as this takes. I want to be able to talk to you or
your team at any time about anything and know I'm not
having to worry about other issues.'

Max stood ramrod straight, his mouth tight as he

stared back. The silence was laden with all the arguments and rivalry of their past. All the current angst and dislike. Then he shoved his hand into Mitch's and they shook. 'Fair enough.'

Mitch felt his twin's warmth through their grasp, and was staggered at the sense of need that assailed him. When had he last touched Max? What would it be like to be able to walk up to him and ask how his day was going? To pick up a phone and suggest a drink at the pub?

Then the surrounding silence trickled into his brain and he looked around to find everyone watching him and Max. Max must've noticed at the same moment because he tugged his hand free and stepped back. But that severe look Max reserved entirely for him had lightened a little.

Ignoring everyone, Max dropped his gaze to Jamie and his countenance softened further. His chin moved down and up in agreement. 'I still can't get my head around the fact I'm an uncle.' Turning a gaze filled with something like need to Mitch, he added, 'Ask me anything you want. I'll always tell you exactly what's going on and where we are at.'

'Fair enough.' More than he'd expected. And yet why? Max was the consummate professional and an exceptionally good surgeon. Even when it came to his own flesh and blood. Especially when it came to his own family. 'Thanks. A lot.'

Very few words and yet he felt as though he'd taken a giant step towards his brother and maybe a slightly brighter future. Could be that Jamie was going to turn out to be the best thing that had ever happened to him in more ways than one. But he'd take things slowly, carefully. There was a long way to go if he and Max were even going to be on easy speaking terms.

He watched as Max tapped the back of Jodi's hand.

'For a moment on Monday I thought you'd lost your toughness, but I was wrong. It's there in loads. Jamie's lucky to have you on his side.'

'You didn't think I'd let this turn me into something as soft as spaghetti, did you?' Jodi gave him one of her megawatt smiles.

'I guess not.' Max smiled his Maitland smile then turned away to face Mitch.

Mitch met his twin's steady gaze and shock slammed into him. Compassion blazed back out of those eyes that mirrored his.

Nah. Couldn't be. Never once in all the years since he'd screamed for Uncle Fred not to take Max away, for Max to turn round and come back to him, had he known anything from Max that might indicate they were on the same side.

Even at their eighteenth birthday dinner with supposedly loving family—the uncles who didn't like each other, the aunts who tolerated one another—the underlying competitiveness between him and his twin had risen to the fore, each being encouraged by their respective adoptive uncle. The evening had quickly been ruined. That had been the last time they'd even pretended to want to get together and be buddies.

And now Max goes and shows empathy for his situation. Mitch looked away, around the group of medical specialists gathered for Jamie, and saw their admiration for his brother. He had to agree with them. Max was very good at what he did for his patients.

Mitch's gaze dropped to his boy. Jamie. Seemed this kid was stirring up the Maitland family all by himself. Might as well get this next bit over before he changed his mind—which in the circumstances would be foolish and selfish. Breathing deeply, he opened his mouth and turned to his twin, told him, 'You're to do the operation when the time comes.'

Jodi gasped. 'Excuse me?'

Guilt assailed him. So much for discussing something as important as who the surgeon would be. Jodi's lips were tight, her eyes spitting at him. He hurriedly said in as placating a tone as he could manage without seeming to grovel, 'We'll talk later.'

She knew Max was the best transplant surgeon available. And they wanted the best.

Max's eyes had widened and he gave Mitch the full benefit of that infuriating twist of his mouth he'd perfected. But his eyes were devoid of anything other than acknowledgement of the statement. He nodded slowly, as though digesting a lot more than the fact he was to do the lifesaving operation on his nephew. 'I hope that won't be too long away.' Spinning away, he gathered his team around him and began an in-depth discussion about Jamie's case before they all moved on to examine a teenager further down the ward.

A chill slid under Mitch's skin as he watched him go. Had his brother already reached the far point of this whole transplant equation? Come to the conclusion that Mitch was going to have to put his hand up and volunteer a kidney? Did Max understand him better than he realised? Why wouldn't he? They were twins, after all. Despite living most of their lives apart in very different circumstances, they knew each other—very well.

Which meant Max totally understood the arguments he was having with himself. Not that he was trying to get out of the situation. He'd already started down the track of finding out if he'd be a suitable donor by getting Lucas to arrange further tests now that he knew the blood types were compatible.

But it was the wider picture that frightened him. The whole thing of committing to helping his son and the ram-ifications afterwards—the ties to his lad that were build-ing day by day, hour by hour. The fear he'd fail Jamie. Nothing to do with giving the kid a kidney and all to do with giving him his heart. And Max, blast him, could see that as plain as day.

'Can Bingo sleep with me?' Jamie's big blue eyes, filled with trust, stared at Jodi.

'Bingo? Is that teddy's name?' Where did he get these names?

'I like Bingo.'

'He's very cute.' A smile tugged at the corners of her mouth as she tucked the teddy bear in beside him. Two days after being rushed into hospital, Jamie was sound-ing more like himself. But he was still tired, which was why he'd snuggled down after his breakfast in prepara-tion to having a nap. There'd be more dialysis treatment later in the day.

'Where's Mitch, Mummy? He hasn't seen me for ages.'

Mitch had been the favourite person in Jamie's life since he'd been handed the big bag and told to take a look at his new friend. Just to see Jamie's eyes popping out of his head had brought warmth curling through her where she'd been cold for the past night and day. Also making Mitch the most favourite person in her life at that moment.

Despite not talking to her about Max doing the sur-gery. That annoyed her, but it was so Mitch. Taking charge was as natural to him as charming everyone he wanted something from.

'Mitch is busy at work but he'll be up to see you soon.' Now she was defending the guy for being at work. Funny how things went round in circles. To think that a few days ago she'd intended to drag Mitch away from that department of his to be with her and their son until this was over, until he saw how ill Jamie was and how desperately his son needed his kidney.

Stretching her legs out to ease a light cramp in her calf muscles, she couldn't help smiling. Now she was happy that Mitch had his work to keep him balanced while he adjusted to being a father and all that involved.

Nothing that Max and his transplant team had discussed with them had made her feel any better. Except, maybe, that they were all agreed that the sooner Jamie had a new kidney the better. It couldn't come soon enough in Jodi's mind, while at the same time she battled the fear of knowing her little boy had to go under the knife.

Mitch had been acting a bit strangely since he'd told Max he had to do the transplant, going vacant on her at inopportune times. Was he finding it hard that he had to rely on his brother to help them? Maybe this could lead these two stubborn people towards some sort of reconciliation. Or was that like wishing every day to be sunny and warm?

While Mitch hadn't intimated so, she felt he was seriously considering the whole kidney donation thing. And while that's what she hoped for and thought she'd be able to ask him to do, being with Mitch these past few days she'd found she just couldn't do it. That it was Mitch's decision alone, and that she had no right to ask such a huge thing of him. Mitch being Mitch, he'd get there in his own way and time.

Max had talked to them about the odds of a kidney becoming available in the near future. Not good. No one had mentioned that it was in the lap of the gods unless Mitch put his hand up to find out if there was any reason why he couldn't donate a kidney. No sign of Mitch doing that, either. Not a dicky bird.

'Mitch,' shrieked Jamie. 'You came.'

'Why wouldn't I, little man? Hmm?' Mitch gave Jamie's hand a squeeze. Then did the same to Bingo. 'Hey, bear, how're you doing?'

Jamie giggled. 'Grandma, look what Mitch gave me.'

Jodi's head spun. Mitch and Mum coming in together? Seemed Mitch was knocking down a few fences at the moment.

Mitch slid a hand onto her shoulder, his fingers gently squeezing warmth into her. 'Hey, there. We've come to sit with Jamie while you go and have a shower, refresh yourself.'

When she looked up at him she noted Mitch was focused on Jamie, his eyes making a rapid medical scan, as all doctors were prone to do. What about fathers? Yep, they tended to do that too even if they weren't medically trained. It was an instinctive thing.

'I've brought you clean clothes, and your shampoo and conditioner.' Mum handed her a small bag before dropping a light kiss on Jamie's cheek. 'Hi, sweetheart. How's my boy? And who's that in bed with you?'

'Bingo.' Jamie tried to lift his new mate but he was too tired. That short burst of excitement had already drained what little energy he had.

'Here.' Jodi reached for the teddy and sat him on top of the bed for everyone to admire.

'Granny, can I have a story?'

'Sure can. I've brought all your books with me. We'll read while Mummy goes and spruces herself up, shall we?' Mum was really laying it on about her looking a mess. If she thought a quick shower and clean baggy jeans and top would impress Mitch, think again. He liked his women looking sensational. Not to mention stylish. For a fleeting moment she thought longingly of all those outfits hanging in the wardrobe of her spare bedroom back in Dunedin.

But, no, her bedraggled appearance was the real her, the newer her. It came with the job of being mother to a sick child. Anyway, she didn't have the energy to care.

Mitch was pulling back her chair and taking her elbow, hauling her up. He handed her a key. 'Go on. This is for the on-call room. It's all yours for as long as you need it. You'll feel better after a relaxing time under those jets of hot water to ease out the cricks and tight spots in your muscles.'

'Sounds delicious.' And too darned exhausting to even walk the distance to wherever this on-call room was. She didn't have the strength to move, let alone argue with these bossy people. Every muscle in her body groaned and her backside aimed for the chair. The drums in her head were playing a heavy beat.

'No, you don't,' Mitch muttered.

She'd have to give it her best effort. 'See you soon, sweetheart.' As she leaned over Jamie to plaster his cute face with kisses the mug of disgusting instant coffee sloshed in her stomach. It was always like this whenever Jamie was in hospital.

'Come on, I'll show you where the on-call room is.' Mitch swung the bag off the floor and waved to Jamie. 'See you in a few minutes, sport.'

'Okay.' Jamie's mouth widened into a huge yawn.

Jodi yawned in sympathy. 'I hope this room isn't too far away.'

'I could find a wheelchair.' Mitch grinned.

The grin disappeared when she muttered, 'I could almost take you up on that.'

An arm came round her waist, holding her upright and close to Mitch's warm, strong body. 'I've put some chicken in the little oven to keep hot for you. Claire's been cooking all morning.' As she opened her mouth to protest he shook her gently. 'Don't even think of saying you don't need food. You do. You're shattered and you haven't eaten since I brought in that panini for breakfast.'

'The thought of food makes me feel ill.'

'You need to keep your strength up for Jamie.'

'Since when did you become such a nag?'

'Just looking out for you.' That grin had returned.

'I know.' She did, truly, but it was too hard.

'In here.' Mitch took the key from her fingers and opened the door for her. Then he followed her in.

'Hey, thanks, but I'll manage from here.' Jodi leaned against the wall. Liar. The moment Mitch walked out that door she'd slide into a heap on the floor. Probably fall asleep right there.

'It's all right. I'm not about to offer to wash your back for you.' Couldn't he look at least a teeny-weeny bit disappointed? 'But I'll pour you a glass of juice and dish up the chicken.'

She dredged up a smile. 'You're going to force-feed me now?' Having those fingers slipping food across her lips would be nearly as good as him washing her back.

'If you don't move soon I'll toss you over my shoulder, march you into that bathroom and put you under the shower.' His eyes widened and that grin slipped a little. 'Except there's less room in there than a mouse needs.'

Her head rolled from side to side as images of Mitch carrying her over his shoulder, his hands on her thighs, filtered through the murk that was her brain at the moment. If only she had the energy. Forcing herself upright, she took a step in the direction of the only other door in the room. 'On my way.'

Mitch looked down into her eyes. 'Just taking care of you. For Jamie.' His head lowered. 'And this is for me.' His lips brushed her forehead, strong and firm yet as light as a butterfly landing on her skin.

Then he stepped back and turned her to face the bathroom door. With a gentle shove he said, 'Go on. You'll feel a lot better afterwards.'

She stumbled into the bathroom and banged the door shut behind her. Leaning back against it, she brushed her forehead with her fingertips. He'd kissed her. Not a proper, lips-on-lips, tongue-circling-tongue kiss but something so sweet and caring that her heart felt as though it might burst with some strange emotion she couldn't identify.

Didn't want to identify.

Knock, knock. 'Jodi, you all right in there?'

No, I'm totally confused by you. About you. 'Couldn't be better,' she lied as she flicked the shower mixer on as hot as it would go.

Letting the water pour over her, through her hair, down her back, over her face, she tried to blank everything out of her mind. But images of a naked Mitch crammed in there with her, his hands massaging her back, took over, dominating her brain. They'd be so squashed into the shower that every movement they made would involve wet skin sliding over other wet skin. Desire unfurled deep inside her, sending heat coursing along her veins to all her extremities and every place in between.

She wanted Mitch. Now. And he was only a couple of steps away, on the other side of that door. She swallowed, trying to dampen down the flames roaring through her passion-starved body. 'Mitch?' she croaked.

She felt the memories of previous showers with him; her body knew exactly how those firm hands would touch her skin, pummel her muscles to replace the aches with hot desire, with a raw need for him.

'Mitch?' His name came out louder than she'd intended. Full of need and love and plain old horniness.

'Did you call me?' The door cracked open two inches.

Yes, no, I don't know. Her knees trembled. Confusion reigned. The gripping exhaustion had to be why she'd uttered his name. Not the best circumstances to be considering this. Better to wait until she'd slept a straight twenty-four hours. Which wasn't about to happen in the foreseeable future. 'Yes, Mitch, I did.'

The door opened slowly and then closed again, this time with Mitch on her side. Even as he twisted the lock shut he was unbuttoning his shirt enough to haul it over his head. 'Is this wise?'

'Probably not but I need you. Really need you.' Was she being selfish?

Not if Mitch's reaction was anything to go by. Gulp. God, he was stunning in his naked glory, his manhood erect. He needed this as much as she did.

Her eyes widened at the majestic sight filling her vision. Dreams had nothing on the real thing. Memories didn't do the man justice. Her stomach tightened to stop the ball of need from exploding through her. How could her throat be dry when she was immersed in all this water?

He squeezed in beside her, pulling the glass door closed behind him. The blue of his eyes smouldered with desire. Whether this was right or not, she'd make the most of the moment. 'I need you so much,' she whispered. 'I've missed you.' Too much information. But she didn't care. Whatever the result was of this, she would not regret it.

Mitch moved and his skin slid over hers just as she'd known it would, teasing, tantalising, unbelievable. The heat that spiralled over her, through her from that first naked touch tipped her into him. And as his hands spread across her backside to pull her even closer she closed her eyes and gave herself up to him. To Mitch, the man she'd never really stopped loving.

His mouth was hungry, devouring her lips, her throat, tracking down between her breasts. When his lips closed over her nipple she shuddered with excitement. Then his teeth grazed her and she gasped.

She was so ready for him. Slipping her hand between them, her fingers found his erection, stroked the length of him, revelling in the silky feel, in his heat.

Rising onto her toes, she pressed hard against him.

'Jodi,' was all he said as his hands on her backside lifted her enough for him to gain access to her centre.

There was so much passion in the way he spoke her name she almost came. His passion twisted around her, branded her. She was his. Always had been.

And then he was slipping into her and her brain couldn't think at all. All she knew were the exquisite sensations dominating her body, overriding everything else, taking her higher and higher until she was floating. 'Mitch, come with me.'

He did, instantly. And she hung on for dear life, crying out his name over and over as her world shattered into lightness around her.

When he could breathe again, Mitch reached around Jodi and flicked the shower off. Keeping hold of her, he edged the door open and helped her out onto the bathmat. Her body was limp and she swayed on her feet. 'Hey, steady.' Knocked her socks off, did he?

'What happened? That was out of this world.' Her mouth curved into that smile he craved.

He had to kiss her. Taste her. Have more of her. And as soon as his mouth touched hers he could feel his body getting excited again. Whoa. Pull back. As much as Jodi had instigated this, he doubted she had the energy for a rerun. He was surprised she'd managed the first round, given that she'd barely been able to stand up when she'd first gone into the bathroom.

The lips under his moved. 'Don't stop.' She shivered.

Mitch reached for a towel. 'You're getting cold, Jodi. Let me dry you off.'

'Cold? I'm burning up.' Her smile widened as another shiver shook her.

'You're good for my ego, woman, but catching a chill isn't such a brilliant idea.' He rubbed the towel gently over her breasts, biting down on the flare of need slamming through him. Finish the job and get her dressed, hide all that flesh before you really lose your head and take her again. 'Turn around,' he growled softly. But the sight of those round buttocks stalled the air in his lungs.

Closing his eyes, he counted to ten, twenty, thirty. Finally his breath eased out and his muscles loosened up a little. 'Here, you're dry. Get some clothes on, will you?'

She didn't have to give him that wicked smirk as she opened her bag to find something clean to wear. Bloody woman, she'd be the death of him. She tugged on underwear and a T-shirt that only came down to mid-thigh—and ramped up his heart rate dangerously high.

Now that he'd made love with her he knew he wanted it again and again. Once was not enough. Jodi was back in his life in another way now. This was one way he knew her well, what he'd missed so much, and wanted for the future.

His head reared up. The future? With Jodi? *Yeah, well, weren't you getting to that? Hasn't the idea been flapping around in your brain for days now? As the shock of learning about Jamie has ebbed you've been more and more aware of Jodi as the woman you once loved.*

Food for thought.

'Time for that chicken,' he muttered, trying desperately to get back on track.

Jodi looked up at him from under her eyelashes and swayed some more. 'Think I'll have a snooze first.'

'Yes, you're asleep on your feet, sweetheart.'

Her eyes widened at that but for once she remained quiet. Not having second thoughts, he hoped. Tugging down the covers, he said, 'Come on. Climb in.'

'Mitch,' she murmured as she snuggled down.

'Ye-es.'

'We've still got what it takes, haven't we?' Her eyes closed and he'd swear she'd fallen asleep on her last word.

'Yes, sweetheart, we have.' He brushed a kiss on her forehead and tucked the sheet under her chin. Then crept out of the on-call room and went to sit with his son.

CHAPTER NINE

THE FOLLOWING AFTERNOON in the ED Mitch gently felt along Mark Williams's arm. 'Any pain where I'm touching?'

The fifteen-year-old nodded. 'Hurts like stink everywhere. That prop was a big guy.'

'You're no midget yourself.' Mitch gave the mud-covered lad a smile. 'Did his head crash into you or his shoulder?' Not that it mattered. The damage was done.

'Think it was his head, but then his whole body slammed on top of me as I went down. Pow. But I got the try.' Mark grinned despite his obvious pain.

'Good for you. Hope your team wins and makes the mess you've got yourself into worthwhile.' Mitch filled out a form requesting X-rays of Mark's humerus and ribs.

'Inter-school rugby matches tend to be physical,' Carl said from the corner.

'All rugby is physical,' Mitch muttered. 'Hang around here on the weekend and see how many bodies we get to patch up.'

'Am I going to be on TV?' Mark grinned at the camera being directed his way.

'You might,' answered Carl. 'Depends on the editing process and what other cases we get over the next couple of days.'

Mitch pulled in a lungful of air. *Yeah, focus on Mark and forget all about Jamie.*

'Cool,' Mark said. 'Wait till I tell my mates. They'll be green.' Then he jerked round to offer a better profile to the camera and groaned in pain.

'Take it easy. You have some broken bones that won't take kindly to sudden movement.' Mitch carefully pressed the boy back against his pillow and glanced across to Samantha. 'Can you arrange for an orderly to take Mark up to Radiology, please?'

Mitch headed to the station where he picked up the next patient file. Turning, he almost bumped into Carl. 'See, plenty of willing patients for you and your crews to make an excellent documentary about.'

'You're right. Mark's rugby accident will resonate with many teenage boys and their parents.' Carl's gaze was steady. 'But nothing like the human-interest story we could have about the head of this department and his very ill son.'

Mitch bit down on an expletive. He still couldn't get used to other people knowing he was a father when a week ago he'd been blissfully unaware himself. At least no one knew that. They might be wondering, since he'd never mentioned his son, and he could almost hear the debates going on about the situation, but he'd leave them to it. He wasn't about to make an announcement to all and sundry that he'd never been told he was a father.

In the meantime Carl was standing there, expecting an answer to his ridiculous suggestion. 'No.'

'So it's all right for us to interview your patients but not all right to interview you as a parent of one of your patients?'

'You've got it in one.' This guy wasn't going to pull the guilt flag on him. He would protect Jamie, and Jodi for that matter, from all the publicity this man's documentary would generate.

Carl shrugged. 'Believe me, I do understand. As I said, if my daughter was going through what Jamie is I don't know how I'd react to a request like mine.'

'Good, then we understand each other.' Mitch pushed past him, on his way to examine Jocelyn Crooks, who'd apparently been found an hour ago lying on her bathroom floor in a dazed state. 'Anyway, Jamie is no longer a patient in this department.' Just so the guy really got it.

'You know my thinking about that.' Of course Carl was right behind him.

'Right from that very first conversation you and I had about your crews coming in here we established that any patient uncomfortable with your presence could request that they be left alone. As a parent I'm exercising that right for Jamie. Leave him be. He and his mother have got more than enough to deal with.' He snapped his mouth shut, his teeth banging together hard enough to vibrate in his ears.

'We'll talk some more later on.' Carl was so damned calm, so sure of himself.

Whereas he could feel his blood heating to boiling point. But he couldn't lay the blame on Carl. The man was doing his job while he himself was struggling to deal with absolutely everything at the moment. What had happened to his busy but orderly life? Jodi Hawke had happened, that's what. Instantly his temper eased. Jodi. Jodi had come to town. And turned his life around. And given meaning to his existence. And woken his heart up, as she had once before.

Surely this time he could manage to do things the right way and not lose her again. Because if Jodi walked out on him a second time he doubted he'd cope half as well as last time, and he'd barely managed then.

Chas poked his head around the cubicle curtain. 'Rescue Helicopter One on way in from Waiheke Island. Touchdown in ten minutes. Sixty-three-year-old male, chainsaw accident, partially severed leg.'

Mitch looked up from reading Jocelyn Crooks's obs. 'Get the on-call general surgeon on the phone. Call the blood bank and have someone on hand for an urgent crossmatch. Let me know the moment the patient is here.'

He glanced across at Carl and saw the guy go grey. 'This one will be messy. If you or your crew can't deal with that, please stay well away.' His staff would have enough to deal with without having to pick up fainting sightseers.

'I'll talk to the cameraman now.' Carl pushed out of the cubicle.

Mitch called after him, 'This could be a good one to follow up on if the man's agreeable. You'd probably get the Department of Occupational Health and Safety to come on board too.'

Carl turned to shake his head at him. 'Nice try.'

I thought so. Mitch turned back to his middle-aged patient. 'Now, Jocelyn, has this happened to you before?' Pretty much everything was normal, including her blood pressure.

'Never.'

'Do you remember what you were doing before you ended up on the floor?'

Jocelyn looked away. 'No.'

Okay, what was going on here? 'Were you alone?'

'I think so.'

'Drinking alcohol?'

She muttered, 'I only had a couple.'

'I see you're on codeine. Alcohol and codeine don't mix.' Why didn't people adhere to the warnings that came with their drugs? Mitch wanted to lecture the woman but what was the point? If this incident hadn't taught her anything then nothing he could say would have any effect.

Sam arrived with an intern in tow. 'Patient's being brought down from the helipad. Rob will take over here for you.'

Mitch filled Rob in on the few details he had about Jocelyn then headed for the chainsaw patient, rolling his tight shoulders. He really needed to go for a run sometime soon. He'd been missing a few of those since Jodi had turned up.

A nurse called from the desk. 'Mitch, Radiology on the phone. You're late for your appointment.'

His chest X-ray. Damn it. 'Can you get me another time, Sheryl? I can't get away right now. But not tomorrow morning.' He was having an arteriogram done on his kidneys then. And he used to think he had a busy life before.

'Is it really Friday already?' Jodi stirred sugar into her coffee. Round and round and round.

Until Mitch reached for her hand, effectively stopping the movement. Removing the teaspoon from her grip and putting it on Jamie's bedside table, he said, 'All day.'

'One day looks exactly the same as the next, or the last one. Except Jamie sometimes looks a little bit better, then he looks terrible and so sick. And then…' Her voice faded away and her teeth nibbled her lip. The continuous rounds of dialysis were distressing for Jamie, even though they did make him feel less sluggish and took away that horrible bloating.

'Lucas said Jamie's got an infection around the cath-eter site.' Worry deepened Mitch's voice.

'A small one. At this stage.' Any infection was too much. Another problem to be dealt with, more drugs to be pumped into Jamie's body.

And suddenly the tears started. She tried to stop them but how did anyone stop a torrential flood? It was one that had been building up for days, beating at her eye-lids to be freed, only held in place by all the willpower she could muster through her fading strength. She'd been determined not to show Mitch any weakness, and afraid that she would never get back up if she gave in to this gripping worry and fear.

Falling forward, she rested her head on the edge of Ja-mie's bed and gave in, no longer able to fight her grief, her anger, her sense of failure for not being able to do more for Jamie. Throw in the guilt for not telling Mitch about Jamie sooner. What a bloody mess.

Mitch lifted her into his arms, holding her as though she was made of spun sugar. Taking her place on the chair, he sat her on his lap. 'Let it go, Jodi,' he whispered. One hand stroked her back, the other cupped her head to tuck her under his chin. 'You've got to let it all out, sweetheart. It's eating you up.'

If only he knew the half of it. How bad she felt about the way she'd treated him. 'I—I'm sorry,' she tried around the lump clogging her throat. 'For everything.'

'Hey, come on. Two can play that game. I could've come home more regularly, been more attentive, come begging you for another chance. So I'm sorry, too. Okay?'

'But—'

'But nothing.' His chin rested on the top of her head. 'You're here now. We're in this together, no matter what.

That's our boy lying there and we'll do all we can for him. And we'll talk over everything, any time.'

'That feels good, really good.' To have someone with a vested interest to share all the horrible medical facts with, to watch over Jamie with, would make a huge difference to her coping mechanism. 'A new beginning.'

Under her cheek Mitch's chest rose high, dropped back. Did Mitch realise his shirt and suit jacket were getting soaked?

'Something like that. New, but different.'

Pulling her head from under his chin, she twisted round to look him in the eye. 'I like that.' She especially liked what they'd done together in the on-call room yesterday. Maybe she could take a shower every couple of hours.

'I passed Max on the way to the canteen earlier. He asked how Jamie was doing. Said he's getting everything in place in case a kidney becomes available.'

They knew he would. The man wasn't going to play games with something this serious. The stream of tears slowed to a trickle as she shook her head. 'Can't do better than Max.'

'You're right.' Not even a hint of the old angst lined Mitch's words. Blimey.

She settled back against that wide expanse of chest. A great place to be—warm and comforting. And the hand still soothing her back brought other memories back. The day she'd had to have her very old cat put down, Mitch had come home early to be with her. He'd held her just like this until the tears had dried up and then taken her to bed and made exquisite love to her to blot out the sadness for a while. And afterwards he'd gone into town to get a miniature rose bush to plant on her cat's grave.

The rose bush she had pruned every year and remembered the cat, deliberately shoving aside all thoughts of Mitch. How could she have been so single-minded about him? Why hadn't she wanted to recall all the wonderful times they'd had together? Ashamed, she craned her neck and placed her mouth on Mitch's. 'Thank you for being you.'

He shifted his mouth to cover hers fully. His arms wound around her, like a safety net, only this time there was an exciting kind of danger in their hold as well. As though there might yet be something for her, for them, if they could only step cautiously and carefully through the minefield they found themselves in.

'A very salty kiss,' Mitch murmured against her mouth. When she made to pull back he added, 'I like salt. Don't you remember?'

'On your fish and chips, yes, but—'

'Shh, you talk too much.' And his lips covered hers again, shutting off anything she might say.

She'd missed this. Lots. Slipping her tongue cautiously into his mouth to find his, to taste him, she felt the mistake she'd made when she'd kicked him out of her life. How could she have given this up? Must have been on something toxic. Because no one in their right mind would deliberately banish from their life a man who could kiss so superbly.

Mitch's hands had somehow worked under her top onto her waist, holding her against his body. Each fingertip scorched her skin, sending out lines of hot desire, filling her body with a longing so strong she shook. Pressing her breasts hard against him, she revelled in the feel of his rapidly rising and falling chest. Her fingers slid through that thick, dark hair, walked over his scalp. And still she wanted more.

Under her backside Mitch's growing need was becoming more apparent. She wriggled and he gasped. Pulling his mouth away, he stared at her from lust-filled eyes. 'Wrong place, I think.'

Heat seared her cheeks as she abruptly returned to reality. Hurriedly standing up, she turned round and smoothed her top down over her bony hips. 'You're right. I don't know what came over me.'

'That's a shame.'

Snapping her head round, she was confronted with Mitch's wide grin as he stood up. Sighing out a laugh, she told him, 'Thank goodness no one caught us.'

His grin disappeared. 'Would that bother you?'

How the heck did she know? It was too soon. There were too many problems facing them. 'If I think about it, it probably does.'

He leaned in and placed a soft kiss on her cheek. 'Then don't overthink it.' Then he was gone, striding out of the room as fast as those long legs could take him.

Picking up the coffee from where she'd put it earlier, she took a sip and shuddered. Cold. She'd get another one. Jamie was still asleep. He wouldn't notice her absence if she was quick.

But she stayed by the bed, staring down at her son, not seeing him. Instead seeing the older version of those blue eyes and dark hair, smelling the pine and spice aftershave that his dad wore, feeling the ripple of well-developed chest muscles under her cheek.

What had she started when she'd called Mitch into the shower yesterday? A rerun of an old, not-so-good relationship? Or a new version of that, with more honesty and understanding to help it along? They'd talked more in these few days about real things concerning both of them than they had in six months when they'd been together.

Did she want to get back with Mitch? There'd been

as many good times as bad, she realised now that she'd let all the memories in and not just selective ones. But if they had any hope of making a success of being together again, they had a lot of things to clear up first.

And before any of that Jamie had to have his transplant and get well.

And she still didn't know how Mitch felt about donating a kidney. Did she have the right to even ask?

How would I have felt in the situation? Truthfully? I'd hate for someone to tell me that.

But Jamie's nephrologist in Dunedin had done exactly that and she hadn't taken offence. It had been a professional move, not an involved, emotional one. Unfortunately the nephrotic syndrome she'd suffered from as a youngster had precluded her being able to give a kidney to Jamie.

No, whatever was going on between her and Mitch did not give her permission to back him into a corner over a very personal decision. She had to wait. Best to hold off on any more of those kisses, then. No more sex in the shower, or anywhere else. Because of the way her body melted when his lips devoured hers, the chances of her brain remaining in good working order were next to none. And then she'd surely spill the words he and she wouldn't want hanging between them.

'Guess we'd better get back to the hospital and relieve Alison,' Mitch murmured against Jodi's throat. It would be so much better to curl his body around Jodi's and hold her throughout the night while she got some sleep. Okay, not only sleep. He wouldn't be able to refrain from making out with her again. His body was warm and languid right now after making love but it wouldn't be long before everything was up and about, wanting more action.

'Mum did say to take as long as we wanted.' Jodi laughed.

He loved it when she laughed. 'But even she knows dinner only involves a couple of hours. Coming back to the house has stretched those into half the night.'

'I doubt she'll be surprised. Mum doesn't miss much. She probably even guessed we'd grab takeaways and head back here.' Jodi winked at him. 'Though you needn't think you're getting out of taking me to dinner at one of those fabulous restaurants down on the Viaduct.' Jodi trailed her fingers through the light hairs on his chest. 'I was really looking forward to that, but somehow we got sidetracked.'

Yeah, the moment he'd thought about them having a deep and meaningful discussion over dinner he'd changed his mind about going to the amazing restaurant he'd chosen. That was for fun, for romance, not for dissecting their past relationship. 'I'll definitely take you there another night. Soon, I promise.' He crossed his fingers briefly.

Jodi chuckled. 'I'll keep you to that.'

'Anyway, you sidetracked me. Not the other way round.'

She blushed. 'I did, didn't I?' Her eyes widened, big brown pools that drew him in. 'I'd decided this wasn't going to happen again. At least not until everything else was out of the way.' The smile she bestowed on him was wicked and cheeky. 'But when you came out of your bedroom looking so mouth-wateringly gorgeous I lost the argument.'

'So why did we get into my four-wheel drive and start heading into town?' It was Jodi who was gorgeous, not him. Dressed in a knee-length dress that floated around her as she moved, the colour—not quite emerald, not quite turquoise—suited her perfectly. His heart had thumped wildly at the sight of her. Wild horses wouldn't have stopped him from kissing her then. And that stunning dress hadn't stayed on very long.

A while later they'd had to get ready all over again, only to get as far as the first Chinese takeout shop before buying some food and racing home again.

'I'd just bought the dress. I had to wear it out somewhere.' Had she thought this might happen when she'd packed it? Her finger circled his nipple. Her tongue replaced her finger, licking slowly, tantalisingly.

Hot need shot through him, waking up every muscle in his body. Again.

'You want more? So soon?' He pushed up on his elbow and leaned over her, kissing those fingers, taking them into his mouth.

'It's this, or having a quick shower and going back to the hospital.' Her hand reached down between his legs. 'Your call.'

It was no contest. Sliding his body over hers, he gave her his answer.

CHAPTER TEN

'Jodi? Can we come in?'

Jodi dragged herself upright from Jamie's bed and ran her hands over her hair and down her face. 'Claire? Of course you can. I'm a bit of a mess but, hey, it's good to see you.' Exhaustion dragged at her muscles, numbed her mind.

Claire stepped closer, tugging a little girl with her. 'I've brought you something for your lunch.'

'You're an angel, you know that?'

'Don't talk daft. How's Jamie doing?' she whispered.

'It's okay, you won't disturb him. He wakes and sleeps as he needs to and no amount of noise will unsettle him.' She stretched her kinked back as she looked at the child hanging on to Claire. 'Hello, you must be Lilly.'

'Lilly Silly Billy.' The girl grinned and shook her head in all directions. 'That's what my friends call me cos I'm always dancing and singing and laughing. Want me to show you a dance?'

Claire quickly cut off that line of thought. 'No, Lilly, no. We're in hospital, remember? Sick people don't like lots of noise.'

'I'd do it quietly, Mum, promise.'

Claire rolled her eyes. 'You don't know the meaning of the word.'

Jodi smiled at Lilly. 'Maybe another time. I know, what about when we're at Mitch's house? Do you go there with your mum sometimes?'

'After play centre I do. Can I see Jamie? Why's he asleep in the morning?' Lilly began climbing up on the bed.

'It was a mistake, bringing you here.' Claire lifted Lilly back down to the floor.

Jodi pushed a chair towards Claire. 'No, I'm glad you dropped by. Lilly's not a problem. It's okay if Jamie wakes up. Truly. A little distraction would be good for him. But, Lilly…' Jodi lifted the girl onto her knees. 'See all those tubes?

'They're stuck to Jamie with plaster.'

'Yes, those ones. Now, you have to be very careful not to bump any of them because you could hurt Jamie if one gets pulled out by accident.' Her heart ached for her boy who, if he woke up, would be gutted that he couldn't play with Lilly. He'd missed out on so many opportunities to have fun with other kids over the years. It seemed so unfair. Sometimes having all the stories in the world read to him just didn't cut it.

'I'll be good,' Lilly assured her earnestly. Then her face split into another wide smile. 'I'm always good, aren't I, Mum?'

Again Claire rolled her eyes. 'Of course you are.' Then she turned to Jodi. 'I dropped your mum off at the airport.'

'You're kidding! Mrs Independence accepted a lift?' Mum held on to her money like it was a lifeline but she also never took offers of help from people she didn't know very well. Oh. 'I get it. She grilled you on Mitch.'

Claire looked uncomfortable. 'A little bit.'

'Mum doesn't do little. All or nothing is my mother.'

She'd changed her flights by a day so that she could sit with Jamie last night. But now she was heading back to Dunedin to check on her shop, but she'd be back in a week.

'You're right. I got a barrage of questions thrown at me. I think she was disappointed when I explained Mitch was my boss and I wasn't prepared to talk about him behind his back. When I added how much I need my job and why, she backed off.' Claire grinned. 'A little. Actually, I like your mum. She cares about you all.'

'Yeah, she does.' Even Mitch.

Claire sat up straighter on her chair. 'Mitch, hi. I've got your groceries in my car. I'll drop them off after we leave here.'

Looking around, Jodi gaped, then smiled at the man standing a couple of metres away, studying Jamie thoroughly. 'Max, what brings you here?' But she knew already. He'd come to check out Jamie, to take another look at his nephew. He'd been doing that regularly since the team consultation.

Claire stared at Jodi. 'Max? Who's Max? This is Mitch.' Then her eyes widened further. 'Blimey, has the guy been using two different names? That could get him into all sorts of trouble.'

'Claire, meet Max Maitland, Mitch's twin. Max, Claire is Mitch's housekeeper.' She'd never had any trouble telling them apart. Max's eyes were set slightly wider, and his smile didn't have that lopsided thing going on that Mitch's did.

'I never knew Mitch had a twin. Or any family, for that matter.'

Max's mouth tightened but he sounded his usual charming self when he spoke. 'Nice to meet you, Claire.' Then he instantly turned those knowledgeable eyes on Jamie.

Actually, no. Try hungry eyes. Now, there was something to think about. Did Max want kids of his own? Why wouldn't he? She'd judged him on Mitch's standards, which was hardly fair. She stood and crossed to Max, gave him a hug. 'I'm glad you came.'

Max returned her hug before gently setting her aside. 'Just keeping an eye on my patient.'

Sure, buddy. 'Not a problem. He's doing fine, if you call having daily dialysis fine. Which I don't.'

'Okay, watching over my nephew. Feel happier?' He chucked her under the chin with his forefinger, a smile lightening his face.

'Absolutely.' More than happy, ecstatic.

Then the smile slipped. 'Jamie hasn't had a lot of fun in his short life, has he?'

'Very little.' She tried to read his eyes but Max had always been good at hiding his true feelings. It was a family trait. Came with the twin gene. Only one way to deal with either Max or Mitch when they did this. Speak bluntly. 'No fresh kidneys on their way from somewhere around the country, then?'

'You'd be the first to know.' He grunted, shoved his hands deep into his pockets. Another Maitland gesture. 'Ever felt you wanted to step outside and knock someone off so you can save your child? Because that's how I've been feeling all week.'

When Claire gasped, Max turned to her with a self-deprecating smile. 'It's all right. I have no intention of spending the rest of my life behind bars. But this is my nephew. It's a whole different ball game now.'

Claire was staring at Max again. 'You and Mitch must cause a lot of problems around here, being so alike and all.'

'We don't work in the same departments.' Then he

shrugged. 'Yes, occasionally I get grumped at by a staff member for forgetting something when it wasn't me they talked to.'

'Bet you two have caused all sorts of trouble over the years.' Claire grinned as she took her daughter's hand and said, 'Okay, come on, Lilly. We'd better go and unpack those groceries before the ice cream melts. You can see Jamie another time.'

Jodi and Max watched them leave, neither saying a word. As Lilly, looking over her shoulder and waving hard, disappeared around the corner, Jodi turned back to her boy, who had slept through everything. Which brought tears to her eyes. Just another little thing he'd missed out on. A visit from a sweet little girl who wanted to be friends. When was this going to end? How was it going to end? Where was Mitch? Suddenly she wanted him there with her more than anything. His arms around her, sharing his strength, sharing her fears. Guarding their son together.

'How have you managed?' Max's shoulders rolled. 'You still look sane. And strong, which I guess answers my question. But to do this on your own? Obviously still stubborn too. You should've told Mitch. Hell, you should've told me,' he growled.

'Too late for this conversation.' Jodi shivered.

'How's Mitch taking it? It must've been a hell of a shock. Is he okay? I know he seems to be stepping up but what's going on inside that skull of his? Does he need to talk to someone?'

Jodi's jaw clenched as she tried not to gasp in surprise at Max's apparently genuine concern for his brother. Totally out of left field. Perhaps Jamie would be the catalyst that got them talking to each other. Really talking, not sniping. 'Maybe you should be talking to Mitch about those things.'

He huffed. 'I'm more concerned about you and Jamie. Mitch is a big boy. He can look after himself.'

'Who's been suggesting I can't?' Mitch snapped from behind them.

'Mitch, no one, not even me, was suggesting you can't,' Max snapped in an identical tone to his twin's.

Mitch studied his brother. 'Okay.'

'I dropped by to see how Jamie was holding up,' Max explained. 'I always feel frustrated waiting for an organ for my patients, but this time it's far worse.'

Mitch nodded. 'Sure is.'

'Mummy.' Right on cue.

'Hey, Jamie, love.' She wrapped his hot little body in her arms and stroked his back.

'Mitch?' Jamie squawked. 'There are two Mitches.'

'No, love. One's Mitch.' One day you'll call him Daddy. 'And the other's Max. You met him the other day.' One day you'll call *him* Uncle Max.

'No, I didn't.'

Okay, not going there. Too complicated. 'Want a juice? Or some water?'

'No.' Jamie yawned and snuggled in against her, his big, bewildered eyes peering out at the two men standing together at the end of his bed. Side by side.

'Thought I might find you here.' Carl strolled into the room, dressed comfortably in jeans and an open-necked shirt. 'Didn't expect to see both the Maitland doctors in the same room together.'

Mitch spun round. 'Carl. I've said no. You are not coming near Jamie or Jodi. Not now, not ever. Which bit of that don't you get?'

Carl held up a hand. 'Take it easy. I'm not here to

badger you or Jodi. I wanted to see how the wee lad was getting on. Nothing more than taking an interest in your child.'

Max turned slowly and eyed the newcomer up and down appraisingly. 'I don't believe we've met.'

The man thrust his hand out. 'Carl Webster, TV Aote-aroa. I'm filming a documentary in this hospital's emer-gency department.'

Jodi wrapped her arms tighter around Jamie. 'Are you still hoping I'll agree to you filming my son?' Her voice was rising. Frantically swallowing, she tried to lower the pitch of her voice. 'The answer is no. Absolutely not. Get it? I know I thought it could be good for the donor ser-vice but I just can't have anyone coming near Jamie with a camera. Not so you can give your viewers some excite-ment while they eat their dinner and argue over whose turn it is to clear the table.'

Mitch came to her, laid a hand on her shoulder. 'Jodi, he won't. Trust me.'

Carl stepped up to the bed. 'Jodi, I apologise for giv-ing you the wrong idea. I genuinely wanted to see how Jamie was. I've overheard conflicting snippets of talk from the staff. I feel for you all. There is no ulterior mo-tive in my visit.'

He had guts. She'd give him that. 'I see.'

Max looked at Jodi, something like sympathy in his eyes. He smiled kindly then read the charts at the end of Jamie's bed. 'He's holding his own. I'll drop in again later.' With that he strolled out of the room, as if he didn't have a worry in the world. But he had been concerned about Jamie. About Mitch, even.

'I'll be getting back to my crew.' Carl turned to fol-low Max then turned back. 'But if there is anything I can do for you, please don't hesitate to ask. I'd really like to help if I can.'

Jodi stared after him, even when he had turned the corner and disappeared from sight. 'I think he meant it.'

'I guess we'll never know. I'm not asking him for anything.' Mitch sat on the edge of the bed. 'How'd you like to go home for the night, Jamie?'

'Ah, excuse me?' Jodi glared at Mitch.

'Wouldn't you like to spend a night in a bed, not sprawled out beside Jamie?' When her eyes widened he smiled. 'On your own, getting some much-needed sleep.'

'Oh.' Disappointment flared. It hadn't taken long to get used to having sex again. But Mitch was right. She did need sleep—very badly.

He was still smiling. 'What about a quiet night without nurses shining torches as they check on Jamie? Not to mention a meal that hasn't been reheated in the microwave?'

'Low blows, Dr Maitland.' She weighed up the pros and cons. It wasn't as though Jamie wouldn't have medical care on hand. 'I guess Jamie's well enough for an overnight stay away from here.'

'We've got Lucas's approval.'

'Stop looking so smug.' Her sprits were suddenly lifting.

'Can I take Bingo home?' Jamie asked.

'Where you go, Bingo goes, sport.'

If only everything could be sorted out as easily.

Mitch put the last pot away and hung the tea towel on the oven door handle. Leaning back against the bench, he folded his arms across his chest and breathed deeply. 'Jodi, how would you feel about us telling Jamie who I really am?'

Her head snapped up so fast it must've hurt. The gaze that met his was filled with surprise. Then she studied him as though she was looking at every single cell of his body.

He waited for all the questions about his intentions. He was ready for her, knowing deep within he'd never back off from being a father to Jamie. Now Jamie was in his life there'd be no letting go, no changing his mind. There were a lot of things to decide still, like Sydney and whether Jodi moved over there with him, but he'd make it all work. He had to.

Jodi smiled. 'I'd like that. He should know.'

'Truly? Just like that?'

'I can see you mean it, that you didn't just decide this between washing the dishes and putting them away in the cupboards. You really care about Jamie, love him, and that's all that matters.'

The tension gripping him eased off. His mouth spread into a smile. Warmth sneaked through him.

'Let's tell him now before I put him to bed.' She pushed up from the table.

Mitch looked through to the lounge where the TV was tuned to a cartoon programme. Jamie lay curled up on the couch, his blankie in his fist, thick pyjamas keeping him snug. Bingo was perched on the arm of the couch. Mitch could feel his heart swelling with love for the little man who carried his genes. Reaching for Jodi's hand, he walked through to his son.

But Jodi took over before he could utter a word. 'Jamie, sweetheart, we've got something to tell you, something good.'

'Not now, Mummy. I'm watching the dogs chasing the rabbits.' Jamie's gaze didn't waver from the screen as he pointed. 'See?'

'I see,' his mother answered, without looking around. 'Jamie—'

Mitch shook his head at her. 'It's okay. Only a few minutes till the end,' he said. 'It's kind of funny, really. When I finally want to tell Jamie I'm his dad he makes me wait for the cartoons to finish.'

He sat down on the other end of the couch, stretching his legs half across the room. He watched the enjoyment flitting across his boy's face and the resulting giggles making his cheeks screw up. Saw the gap where Jamie had lost a tooth this week. Noted the dark too-long hair so like his own. The tiny scar on his chin where Jodi said he'd once banged into the corner of a table. The little-boy things that made Jamie who he was.

Sitting beside him on the arm of the couch, Jodi swung her legs and played the piano on her thighs with her fingers.

Suddenly Mitch's stomach squeezed. Was this the right time to be telling him? Why not wait until after the surgery? But almost immediately the panic abated and he relaxed again. He wanted this.

The credits began to roll on the screen. 'Finished, Mummy. Can I have a drink?'

Jodi leapt off the couch and went to kneel beside Jamie. 'In a minute. Do you know what a daddy is?'

Jamie nodded. 'He's a man-mummy.'

Mitch felt his mouth drop open. *I'm a man-mummy? Couldn't have put it better myself.* And he grinned.

Jodi blinked and swallowed a laugh, but the look she shot him was one of pure fun. 'Jamie, Mitch is your daddy.'

At least she didn't say I'm his man-mummy.

Jamie looked over at Mitch and shrugged. 'Okay.'

'You can call him Daddy now, not Mitch anymore.'

'Okay. Can I have my drink now?'

Mitch stared at this kid whom he'd fathered. Who'd taught him to be so offhand? If he hadn't known better he'd have thought he'd been around Jamie all his short life. Well, he, for one, was changing. 'Hey, Jamie, want a hug first?'

'Yes, please. I like hugs.'

And when small arms wound too tightly around Mitch's neck, he grinned. 'So do I, Jamie. So do I.'

'Phew. For a moment there I thought we were in for an argument.' Shock receded from Jodi's eyes, replaced by love for her boy. 'But he came through. As he always does.' She scrubbed her eyes with the back of her hand.

Mitch was torn between holding the squirming bundle in his arms and reaching for Jodi to haul her against him. Somehow he managed to juggle Jamie and snag his mother. They sat in a squashed heap on the couch holding on to each other until Jamie wriggled out. Which was almost immediately.

Mitch didn't care. His heart was bursting. He'd done something right for Jamie. And himself. Another step ticked off. Except this one was so huge. Was this how mountaineers felt? Exhilarating now the worry was over, huh?

'Man-mummy, want a coffee?' Jodi asked as she extricated herself from his hug.

'Watch it,' he growled, trying to hold in a laugh and failing. As the laughter rolled out of him he felt the best he'd done in a very long time. Since the day Jodi had dumped him. Yeah, he could get used to all this commitment stuff after all. So far it hadn't hurt a bit.

Still feeling the effects of a good night's sleep, Jodi wandered out into the kitchen in her thick pyjamas and warm bathrobe, looking for a cup of tea.

'Hi, sleepyhead. Thought you'd never wake up.' Mitch sat at the table with Jamie on his knee getting stuck into a plate of toast and honey.

'Hi, Mummy. Mitch let me make my own toast.'

'That explains the honey on your forehead.' Jodi kissed his cheek. And got a whiff of delicious aftershave. Hurriedly stepping away, she busied herself with filling the kettle, finding a mug and the teabags. Too early in the morning for thinking about sexy men. Gees, showed how bad things were. There had been a time when it was never too early. Or too late, come to think of it. 'So you're still Mitch, then?'

He shrugged, apparently totally unfazed. 'Better than man-mummy.'

'You should've woken me. You'll be late for work.' She yawned and stretched her arms high above her head.

Mitch's gaze seemed stuck on her chest. 'It's Saturday. I'm not going in.'

The mug banged down on the bench. 'What?' Was he all right? Never had Mitch not gone to work on the weekend. Saturdays and Sundays were just normal days in his book.

'I've got more important things to do than look after patients today.' He sounded so smug.

Grabbing the milk from the fridge, she poured some into the tea and dropped down on a chair before her legs gave out in shock. 'What's more important than your department?'

'My son. And my son's mother.' Definitely smug. And smiling. 'You never thought you'd hear me say that, did you?'

'Honestly? Not before aliens took over the planet.' The tea scalded her tongue. Damn. 'Okay, spill. What's going on?'

'Jamie's got dialysis at ten.'

'Ye-es?'

'You've got an appointment in Parnell at nine-thirty.'

'I have? Since when? You've got the wrong woman, surely?' Weirder and weirder. She held up her hand in a stop sign. 'Mitch, did you take something you shouldn't? Should I be taking you to get your stomach pumped out?'

Jamie wriggled off Mitch's knee and took his plate over to the bench, reaching high to get it over the edge. Jodi automatically reached too, and saved the dish. When she sat back and reconnected with Mitch she saw his gaze had focused on her chest again. Glancing down, she muttered under her breath and tugged her robe closed over her breasts.

Mitch stood and began clearing the table of crumbs. 'I thought I'd take Jamie for his appointment while you go to a spa. The Indulgence Spa, actually. I've booked you a half-day session, longer if you want it.'

It was hard to talk when her mouth was hanging halfway to her knees. 'A spa?' Her? When was the last time she'd pampered herself? How old was Jamie? Three years four months and some days. That's how long ago.

Mitch towered over her, tilting her head back with his finger under her chin. 'If you really don't want to go then I won't argue. But before you say flat out no, think about it. You're exhausted.'

She nodded. 'But that only means I'll fall asleep on the massage bed.'

Mitch ignored her. 'I doubt you've done anything for yourself in all the time since Jamie was born. I want you to feel better within yourself, to luxuriate with a massage, facial and any other woman thing you want.'

That was quite a speech. 'Thank you, but I always go with Jamie for his treatments.'

'Jodi.' Mitch lowered his head to brush her mouth with his lips. 'He'll be fine with me. I am a doctor. More than that, I'm his father and I'm trying to be one. You have to let me do things like this.'

'That includes looking out for me, too?' The moment she'd spoken her lips sought his again. Finding them, she pressed up against him. How had she survived all this time without these lips to kiss, lips that teased and tormented, caressed and heated her up?

'You're part of the deal. Jodi and Jamie.' He leaned into the kiss, opening under her mouth, his tongue slipping across hers. His hands gripped her shoulders holding her in place. He needn't have worried. She wasn't going anywhere.

'Mummy, what are you doing?' Jamie tugged at the belt on her robe and she jerked away from Mitch whose eyes were filled with laughter.

'I'm kissing him.' That's what mummies and daddies did in an ideal world. Not as good as the whole works—commitment, love, sharing. 'It's a start.'

'It sure is,' said a bemused Mitch from the other side of the kitchen, where he'd suddenly become frantically busy running water into the sink. Then he twisted the tap off and turned to face her, his face now completely serious. 'I don't know what you want from me other than to be a part of Jamie's life. I haven't thought that far ahead yet. But you can believe me when I say I accept my role in Jamie's life. I am his father and nothing is ever going to change that. Nothing will take that away from me.'

CHAPTER ELEVEN

JODI SCRAPED THE roast lamb and vegetables off her plate into the rubbish bin. The racket made by dropping the plate and cutlery into the sink jarred her teeth, and cranked up her temper even more.

'You haven't changed one bit, Mitchell Maitland. All this talk about wanting to help me, to be there for Jamie, and where are you now? Dinner was ready two hours ago.'

All that pampering at the spa last weekend did not make up for this. All the sweet words, the kind gestures, doing the involved-father acts did not make up for his lateness.

'You could've at least phoned or texted.' Yeah, right.

She'd gagged, trying to swallow a mouthful of the delicious-smelling dinner she'd prepared. After waiting an hour and a half, giving him the excuse that he really had got caught up in an emergency at work, she'd carved a slice of the succulent meat and spooned gravy over that and the vegetables. But the moment she sat at the carefully laid table her stomach had started churning. Not wanting to let Mitch win, she'd forced her teeth to chew, her throat to swallow. She hadn't got past that first taste.

Covering the rest of the meat, she left it to go cold. The vegetables looked soggy and flat in the cooled roasting pan sitting on the stovetop. She lifted them onto a plate to set aside. The pan went into the sink to soak.

'Note to self: don't ever think you can prepare a meal for Mitch that he's going to sit down and eat with you on time.'

She flicked the kettle on. Maybe tea would be okay in her delicate stomach.

'Second note to self: remember the lessons learned the first time you had anything to do with Mitchell Maitland.'

The teabag steeped in the boiling water. Jodi tried to swallow the disappointment that had engulfed her but that was as hard to do as swallowing her dinner. Had she expected too much of Mitch?

She nudged the teabag with a teaspoon, squished it before removing it. Stirring in milk, she stared at the murky liquid. Not very appetising but better than nothing. Unlike Mitch. Very appetising but definitely not better than nothing.

'Third note to self: don't fall in love with him all over again.'

She dropped the teaspoon on top of the dirty plate and taking her mug in a shaky hand she headed for Jamie's bedroom. Her heart was squeezing, fit to bust. Her lungs were struggling to do their job. Just before her brain closed down on this bleak discussion it added one more warning.

'Fourth note: it's too late. Too bloody late. You're already completely in love with him.'

Mitch leaned his elbows on the railing and peered down into the dark sea metres below, his hands clasped tightly in front of him, his fingers feeling as though they'd never straighten again. The wind tossed spume in the air and across his face. His tongue tasted salt on his lips. He was impervious to that and the rain running down his neck. The anorak wasn't doing its job. In the scheme of things, getting wet didn't even register.

On the road behind him cars whizzed through the puddles, horns blared as impatient drivers hogged the road. Thursday-night clubbing and drinking awaited them. All so darned unimportant.

He was compatible. With Jamie. In every essential aspect.

The tissue typing showed no problems with their white cells. The crossmatch had come up negative, telling him that Jamie wouldn't reject his kidney. The X-rays showed all was good inside, and the arteriogram showed his renal system was in superb working order.

Jamie could have one of his kidneys. Any day now.

Which was good. Great, even.

The relief was huge. His boy would be safe, could start to live a normal life for the first time. Whether that life was in Dunedin or Sydney had yet to be sorted, but he wasn't overly concerned. Somehow he and Jodi would make that work. Even if he had to give up the new job. That idea didn't gut him as much as it would've a few weeks back.

So what's your problem?

That was the problem. He didn't know. Couldn't say why he felt so drained, so unexcited. When Lucas had given him the good news he'd been thrilled. At last he was going to do something worthwhile for his family. Because, unmarried, not together, Jodi was his family as much as Jamie.

So if that's how you feel, shouldn't you be at home, telling her the good news? Celebrating with a glass of wine and watching her face light up with wonder? Seeing that worry and fear slip away from those sad brown eyes?

Too right. He'd even bought the champagne on the way home, before he'd turned round and headed out here to think. The good mood had evaporated, leaving him with more questions than ever.

Did people celebrate donating one of their kidneys to their son? Or was the situation too grim for that?

Jodi would be relieved at the news. More than relieved. This was what she wanted, what she'd come to Auckland and him for. He'd known it the moment he'd heard the word 'cystinosis'.

Not that he could find fault with her over that. Their son's life was at stake. Of course she'd do whatever was necessary. Even knock on his door.

But what if after the transplant Jodi didn't need him to be a part of her life? What if that was all she'd wanted from him and the kisses and lovemaking had been incidental? Or just a big mistake? She'd never stop him seeing Jamie. He knew that as well as he knew anything.

I definitely do not want to be a part-time dad, having Jamie to stay in the holidays, spending every second Christmas with him, flying to Dunedin for his birthday.

More than that, he wanted Jodi in his day-to-day life. Not as his child's mother but as his partner, his wife. His lover. His friend.

He loved her. *I love Jodi Hawke.*

That had been creeping up on him since she'd dropped back into his life. There hadn't been any fireworks blinding him. No clashing cymbals awakening his heart. No, the realisation that he loved, still loved, her had been a slow slide in under his skin to take over his mind.

Right now he didn't know what to do about his love.

He wanted to marry her, have the whole enchilada, not just the hot sex on the nights they were actually at the house and when Jodi wasn't so tired she fell asleep the moment they finished. He didn't want to have their relationship deteriorate into passing in the hallway of his totally impersonal house as they went their separate ways.

But to tell her this, at the moment, might backfire. He was between a rock and a hard place. He could see Jodi misinterpreting his kidney donation as a way to win her back when the truth of it was he'd never wanted to lose her in the first place.

Stick to the plan, boyo. One step at a time. Everything will work out in the end.

Water trickled down his spine. He shivered and his skin rose in chilly bumps. The next step should be to go home and get into some dry clothes. He smiled as he popped the locks on the car Aaron had lent him for the night. Home to share his news over a glass of champagne and the meal Jodi had said she'd be cooking.

He could almost taste the roast as he turned into the driveway. That sense of homecoming that had gripped him on Jodi's first night in his house washed over him as he noted the lights shining through the gloom, beckoning him inside where it would be warm and cosy. Where hopefully his son slept and Jodi waited, ready to serve up dinner.

Pushing the front door open, he inhaled the delicious aroma permeating the house. His mouth watered as he headed down the hall to the kitchen. 'Hey, Jodi, that's smells wonderful. You're spoiling me. I could get used to this.'

Silence greeted him. 'Jodi?'

The lounge was in darkness. The dining room lights were on and the table set for two. Candles in the middle, wine glasses gleaming. A quick glance around the kitchen told him all he needed to know. He was in trouble with Jodi. *Big time, boyo. You're late home, just like always.*

Except this was different. He hadn't been working, hadn't used patients as an excuse not to come home. He enjoyed coming home these days. She wasn't playing fair. Especially when he had the best news imaginable to share with her.

'Jodi,' he called as he strode towards his bedroom. 'Jodi, where are you?' Disappointment warred with anger as he strode through the door, snapping on the light as he went. 'We've got to talk. Now.'

His bed was empty. A deep chill, colder than that from his wet clothes, bit into him. She'd gone? No, she wouldn't take Jamie out in this weather if she didn't have to. Unless he'd taken a turn for the worse. And then she'd have called.

Mitch spun round, began to stride back to the kitchen. Stopped in the middle of the hall. Jamie's bedroom door was firmly closed. Something Jodi didn't do unless she was in there with him because she was afraid she wouldn't hear him if he became restless or cried out.

His hand shook as he cracked the door open.

Jodi shot up in bed, reaching for her thick robe to keep warm. Her boiling anger had died away to a slow, cold throb as she'd lain there unable to fall asleep. 'Be quiet. You'll wake Jamie,' she hissed. 'He's very restless tonight.' Like mother, like son.

'Then can you come out here so I can explain why I'm late?'

Did he have to sound so reasonable? Had she made a terrible mistake? 'You'd have to have a very good reason.' Now she sounded like a fishwife. But she was so damned angry with him.

'I do.'

'Cellphone not working?' she snapped, barely remembering to whisper. But she did climb out of bed, careful not to disturb Jamie. Keeping as far away from that heart-stopping body as she possibly could, she slipped past him and headed for the lounge. Why was she even giving him the time? She'd heard all this before. The old leopard-doesn't-change-its-spots thing.

In the centre of the room she spun round. 'I don't want to hear how busy it was at work. I know you're the best specialist they've got. I know you're addicted to working every hour there is. Hell, you'd work fifty hours a day if there were that many. But, Mitch, haven't you proved to yourself yet that you're good, that you can do whatever's required of you without foregoing a life? What drives you to be so single-minded about what you do?'

She stopped her tirade. Not because she'd run out of steam. There was plenty more where that had come from. But Mitch wasn't answering back, wasn't defending himself. He hadn't followed her into the lounge.

Instead he stood at the door. Just stood there, not leaning against the doorframe, not folding his arms across his chest as he often did. As though he was waiting for her to have her say and shut up. No emotion flickered over his still face. Nothing showed in those intense blue eyes. So still, so quiet.

So not like Mitch.

A ripple of fear caused her to shiver. 'Mitch?' His silence got to her, started her off again. 'What? No answers? Because I'm right? And here I was thinking you'd changed, that you wanted to be a part of something bigger than just you. A relationship, relationships.'

He sighed.

And she shut up. She'd spewed her guts and he'd sighed. Where was the Mitch who raced to give her all the excuses under the sun? This guy had sighed when she'd read him the Riot Act. Had she got it all wrong? If she had then she'd just blown any chance of them ever getting together again.

'Mitch,' she croaked.

His steady gaze fixed her to the spot. 'Thought you'd like to know that I've found out I can donate a kidney to Jamie.'

All the air in her lungs hissed out over her lips as she collapsed in on herself. Squeezing her eyes shut, she tried to exorcise that image of Mitch as he told her what she'd wanted to hear for weeks. But she couldn't get his face out of her head. His totally emotionless expression pressed at her.

A kidney for Jamie. From his father. And she hadn't even known he was getting the tests done. Because he'd wanted to find out first? Whichever way it went?

Jodi sank to the floor, her legs unable to hold her upright. She wanted the ground to open up and swallow her for ever. Mitch was doing the most generous thing possible for his son. And she'd been ranting and raving at him for coming home late. When had she become such a witch? Had Jamie's illness taken over every part of her so that *she* was the single-minded person she'd accused Mitch of being?

Dragging her head up, she met Mitch's steady gaze. 'I am so sorry, Mitch. I didn't think, didn't consider you might have another reason for not coming home as you'd promised. I'm so sorry,' she repeated.

'We have an appointment with Lucas at eleven tomorrow to discuss what we're doing next, when we might schedule the operations. I'll see you there. In the meantime, I have a job to get back to.'

As Mitch turned away, Jodi noticed a bottle of champagne in his hand. She gasped. Never, ever had she got something so wrong. And the consequences were huge.

She'd just lost the only man she'd ever loved, still loved. Again.

At five to eleven the next morning Jodi was pacing the general waiting room outside the surgical consultants' rooms. Every time the swing doors opened she looked up expectantly. When a stranger walked though her stomach dropped, and she went back to pacing.

Jamie sat sprawled sideways in the wheelchair Mitch had arranged for him, half-asleep, his blankie tucked around him. Since learning he had to go to see the doctor today he'd been grizzly but his lethargy had finally quietened him.

Eleven o'clock clicked over to one minute past on the wall clock. Where was Mitch? And Lucas? According to Lucas's nurse, he hadn't arrived on the floor yet.

She wouldn't even begin to think anything other than that Mitch would be here as soon as he could get away from his department. And that he'd put Jamie first unless it was absolutely imperative for a patient that he stay in the ED.

The doors swung wide and Lucas marched in, Mitch at his side looking quite cool and calm in his perfect suit with matching shirt and tie.

'Hey, sport.' Mitch crouched down by Jamie. 'How's my boy?'

'I want to go home.'

'As soon as we've talked with Dr Lucas, okay?'

Jodi's heart twisted at the love for Jamie emanating from Mitch's face. He had taken this whole situation from a place of shock and horror to something vibrant and caring. How had Mitch done it? It must've taken a massive amount of courage.

'Morning, Mitch,' she said quietly.

'Morning, Jodi.' He dipped his head abruptly in her direction before pushing Jamie's chair after Lucas. 'Let's get this under way.'

'Daddy, I don't want to see that man.'

What? Now? Shock slammed Jodi and she stumbled.

Mitch gaped at Jamie, then leaned down and brushed the hair out of Jamie's eyes with the gentlest of movements. A quick glance at her showed shock and delight mingled in his beautiful blue eyes. Then he straightened up and continued pushing Jamie towards Lucas's office.

Jodi followed in a daze. Jamie had called Mitch Daddy for the first time. Why today, of all days? He'd had days to start saying Daddy and until now she'd not heard the slightest acknowledgement from Jamie that he understood Mitch's special place in his life.

Lucas let Mitch push the wheelchair through to his office before turning to Jodi. 'Are you all right, Jodi?'

'Of course. Jamie's got a very real chance now.'

Lucas caught her elbow to stop her moving forward. 'I don't know anything about the situation between you and Mitch other than you haven't had a relationship for a few years.'

'That's true.' If you didn't count the recent mind-blowing sex. Or that they were sharing his house. Make that had been until last night. Mitch must've slept over here because he hadn't come home at all during the night.

Lucas jiggled her arm. 'I'm probably speaking out of turn—no, I am definitely interfering—but it's important. Please give Mitch some space while he works through this. It's a huge undertaking to donate an organ and while he's willing to do it there are going to be moments when he'll wonder if he's going to be all right afterwards.'

'I understand.' It was great that Mitch had Lucas batting for him. And a shame that he thought she'd be impatient with Mitch while they got everything under way.

'And, Jodi...' Lucas paused and locked eyes with her. 'I'm thrilled for you and Jamie. There's sunshine coming for you. Now, let's get this show on the road.'

It was the first ever medical discussion about Jamie that Jodi sat through without saying a word unless asked a direct question.

She listened carefully as Lucas explained that Mitch would have some sessions with a counsellor before he signed the paperwork required. They discussed how long all this would take, but Lucas hoped to fast-track the last few ends that needed tying up.

'Then,' Lucas added, 'before you get totally excited, there's one final round of blood tests to be done before we go to Theatre. More often than not we don't find any problems at that stage. We'll have covered all the bases in the previous tests.'

Jamie grizzled as Lucas checked him over once more but with Mitch making faces at him and Lucas talking softly Jamie was soon smiling.

Jodi felt estranged from them all. Like she was in a vacuum. She'd got what she'd come to Auckland for: help to save Jamie's life. More specifically she'd got Mitch to offer his kidney. And yet it was as though she'd made a terrible mistake. Not for getting Jamie what he needed— hell, she'd even got him a father. But she'd lost Mitch. Really lost him for good this time. And there was only one person to blame. Herself.

The appointment seemed interminable but at last she

was standing and pushing Jamie's wheelchair out of the small room. Mitch held the swing door open for her. He walked beside her down the long corridor to the lift. He pressed the buttons for the floors they both required. At level one he stepped out the moment the doors slid open.

Jodi watched his stiff gait, saw his hands clenching at his sides, and reached out to him with her hand. 'Mitch.'

He stopped, turned to face her. 'Yes?'

Whatever she'd been about to say froze in the chill pouring off him. Her mouth dried, her tongue stuck to the roof of her mouth. Her arm dropped to her side, effectively letting the doors close and the lift continue its downward journey. Down to the underground car park where she'd left Mitch's vehicle in his reserved slot.

Strapping Jamie in to his seat, she proceeded to take them back to Mitch's house, where Mitch's cleaning lady had country music blaring and the laundry flapping in the winter wind.

Inside the house she tucked Jamie into bed in Mitch's spare room and went to make a strong coffee with beans she'd bought the other day—one of the few things she'd contributed, and that had been more about her than Mitch.

Claire filled another mug and joined her in the dining room, where weak sunlight cut through the windows to create a semblance of warmth. Not that it reached the cold rock that was Jodi's heart.

'Hey.' Claire dropped heavily into a deep armchair, miraculously not spilling a drop of her coffee. 'You look pooped.'

That was putting it mildly. 'Try blind with lack of sleep.' The lethally strong coffee hit her stomach, sent her caffeine-craving senses into raptures. And set the drums in her head beating again.

'Mitch's starting to look a bit like you these days. Like

you're both space trekking.' Claire sipped her well-milked coffee and winced. Her focus appeared to be on the small spider's web in the corner of the room. 'I used to think he ran on empty all the time and still managed to come up looking fabulous. But not anymore. When I saw him yesterday he looked like crap.'

Rub it in, why don't you? 'I'd say it's the worry about Jamie that's doing that.'

'You're probably right. He's used to working all those hours and dealing with everyone else's emergencies, not his own.'

Jodi stared at the woman. Had she been talking to Lucas by any chance? Of course she hadn't. But two similar messages in one morning? Didn't they get it? She knew she'd messed up big time. What she didn't know was how to fix it. None of them had any answers there. 'It's not the same looking after someone who's a patient as it is looking after your own child.'

Claire changed the subject. Slightly. 'Fancy Mitch having a twin brother. It freaked me when you called him Max. I thought you were having me on.'

'That happened a lot at med school.'

'Did you ever make a mistake?' Claire grinned. 'Ever think you were with Mitch when it was actually Max?'

'Not once. I know the difference between Mitch and Max.' Max, who only the other day had told her she was strong. Because she fought for her son. So why wasn't she fighting for Mitch?

The phone in the kitchen rang. 'For you,' Claire said moments later. 'It's Mitch.'

Mitch was phoning her? Her heart rate lifted. 'Hi, Mitch. That was a positive meeting with Lucas.'

'I'm calling to inform you I'm flying to Sydney on

Friday for two days. I'll email you my contact details so
that you can reach me if something happens with Jamie.'

Sydney and his prestigious job. Of course. How silly
of her to forget that.

Mitch dropped his phone on his desk and ran his hands
over his stubbly chin. 'Going to the pack, boyo.'

'Talking to yourself now.' Aaron stood in the doorway.

'Come in and take a pew.' Mitch waved at him. 'You
sure this is all right? Me disappearing for a couple of
days?'

'No worries.' Aaron turned the chair around and strad-
dled it. 'How'd the meeting go with the boss?'

The big boss. 'It's going to work out just fine.' For
who? Him? Jamie? Or Jodi?

'Good. I like what you're doing. For purely selfish reasons, of course.' Aaron talked shop for a bit then stood
up. 'Coming to the farewell bash the TV crew are putting
on? It looks impressive. Probably because they overstayed
their welcome by a week.'

'I guess I'm expected to. At least that's one thing done
and dusted.' Thankfully Carl had seen reason and stopped
harassing him about doing a clip on Jamie.

'Then shift your butt. Kick-off is in thirty minutes.
You could do with some spit and polish before then. Can't
have the HOD turning up looking like something the dog
chewed. They'd probably film you just for the hell of it.'

Mitch rolled his eyes. 'Bloody chirpy, aren't you?'

'Got what I want, didn't I?'

Mitch flapped a hand at his colleague, and the guy
who'd become a good friend. 'Get out of here. I'll see
you shortly.'

'I'll come looking for you if you're late.'

'Getting far too clever for your own good, Dr Simmonds,' he called at Aaron's rapidly disappearing back.

Aaron flipped him the bird and continued down the corridor.

Mitch unfolded himself from his chair and stretched his back, easing the kinks in his spine. Jamming his hands into his trouser pockets, he crossed to the window to stare out at the busy street below. End-of-day rush hour traffic queued for lights, going nowhere in a hurry.

Last thing Friday he'd fly to Sydney. A quick trip. If everything went to plan he might even make a flight back late the next day. The thought of being out of the country when Jamie could take a turn for the worse worried him more than anything. But he had to go. No way around it. Not and keep his reputation from being ripped to shreds.

'What does your rep matter if you don't have the two most important people back in your life?'

He'd worked too hard to let it go easily, even if it wasn't the most important aspect of his life anymore.

He muttered to himself, 'You're working at keeping Jodi and Jamie around for long? Or just until the operation is over and done with?'

No, that was only the beginning of everything. Jamie would be well, able to do all the things little boys did. The kid would have a future, a long future. He'd be able to grow up and decide what he wanted to be as an adult.

'There'll always be the side effects of anti-rejection drugs.' He continued his monologue.

A small price to pay for Jamie's life. As long as someone explained it all to him thoroughly and often. Mitch pinched his lips together.

'That's my role. Among others.' From now on, Jamie had a dad. A father who was never going to leave him to grow up with another male figure. A father who'd put his child first, over everything else.

'And Jodi?'

Yeah, well. Lots of work to do there. Did he even want to try? Risk not being believed, not being listened to and actually heard?

Jodi had cut him right through to his heart with her accusations about not coming home when he'd said he would. It wasn't that she'd made a mistake that got to him. It was that she hadn't given him the opportunity to explain first. Neither had she believed he might've changed.

Hell, when it came to Jamie he'd got up to speed in a very short time. Accepting that Jamie was his. No questions asked. Okay, not many. After the initial shock he'd had no doubt that the boy was his.

And he'd put his kidney on notice for Jamie. Which was what Jodi had wanted all along. What was a guy supposed to do? Beg forgiveness for an argument that was three years old?

Whether Jodi noticed or not, he had changed. Was still changing. He was making plans for the future that involved all of them. Those plans would continue.

CHAPTER TWELVE

JODI'S CELLPHONE VIBRATED on her hip, waking her from a doze. Tugging it free, she read 'Mitch calling' and flicked the phone open.

Exhaling a deep breath, she said, 'Hello. You got my text?' In her worried frame of mind she'd feared it mightn't have reached Mitch in Sydney.

'How bad is he?' Blunt and to the point. No change there.

Jodi glanced at Jamie lying with tubes seemingly coming out of every aperture he had, and then some. The white hospital sheets made him look paler than he already was. 'He's got a fever, higher temperature than last time we were here. He's been on dialysis all day and it doesn't look like Lucas will stop that for a while yet. Basically he's getting worse and there's no stopping it.' She knew the despair in her voice would reach him and that made her feel guilty. But she couldn't help it.

'Hang in there, Jodi. Everything will work out. I promise.'

How can he promise that? 'Sure.'

'I'll get home as soon as possible.'

'Mitch, wait. Do what you have to do. Getting back a day earlier isn't going to change anything here.' Except give me the strength and courage to carry on watching over my boy.

'I want to be with Jamie. And you. I'm missing you both.'

Really? Missing me? Mitch had said that? 'Um, great. Looking forward to your arrival.' *I'll be counting the hours, except I haven't a clue what flight you're booked on.* 'What time tomorrow do you get in?'

The dial tone answered her. He'd hung up. Right. Okay. Now what? Mitch was heading home to Jamie—and her. Did that mean he'd give her a chance to apologise properly? Would he give her a second chance?

She hoped so because she had news for Mitch. Once Jamie had his transplant and had recovered, they were moving to Sydney, too. If possible she'd find a flat near Mitch so he could spend lots of time with Jamie. She'd get work at a local medical centre. And they could both take active parts in raising their son.

'Go to the on-call room and get some decent sleep.'

For a moment Jodi thought Mitch had got back early. She lifted her head and blinked in the half-light of a ward full of sleeping patients. 'Max?' In her dazed state his deep voice had sounded so like his brother's. 'What are you doing here?'

'I heard Jamie had been readmitted.'

'So you wanted to check up on him?' Cool. Max couldn't deny he was an uncle. All the right instincts seemed to have kicked in.

'Seriously, go and grab something for dinner, then put your head down for a while. I'll sit with Jamie until Lucas finishes surgery, which should be by eight o'clock.'

'What has Lucas and surgery got to do with Jamie?' Had she missed something here?

'Lucas says you need a break and there's no one else to sit with Jamie so he's coming as soon as he can.'

Huh? Mr Lucas Harrington was going to sit with her boy for a few hours? 'Heck. He doesn't have to do that.' She studied Max. 'Neither do you.'

'Can't have people thinking Maitlands are no good at looking out for their own. Jamie's my family, too.' He gave her an eloquent shrug. 'I know that much.'

Cool. But—

'You look whacked. Don't want Mitch seeing you like this.' Max sat on the end of the bed and reached to brush her hair out of her eyes. 'Do you trust me with Jamie?'

'Why wouldn't I?'

'Then why are you still here?'

The pillow was soft and tucked around her neck to keep the cool air out. The sheets were heavy and crisp. Luxury after sleeping huddled in a chair by Jamie's bed last night. She rolled on her side and tucked her knees up, wrapped her arms across her breasts.

Half an hour more and then she'd relieve Lucas. Or was it Max? Her eyelids dropped shut.

Mitch immediately wandered into her mind. Laughing Mitch with Jamie, holding his boy ever so carefully. Angry Mitch walking away with a bottle in his hand. Mitch with his feet up on his desk snoring as though there was nothing in the world that could disturb him, only to wake up to hell.

She yawned and stretched her legs, pulled the covers tighter and snuggled further down into the bed. If only Mitch was here now to hold her while she slept, or to make love to her. Those strong yet gentle hands on her skin would stroke her alight, would take her places where all the worries couldn't follow for a short while.

That muscular body would slide over her as he entered her and she could feel his heat, her heat mingling.

Oh, Mitch.

A hand rocked her gently. 'Hey, Jodi, wake up.' A persistent voice from her dream spoke too loudly.

She blinked, snuggled back into the pillow.

'Jodi.'

What? Mitch? For real? Not a dream? She sat straight up, and Mitch had to jerk back to avoid their heads clashing. 'You're not due back till later.'

'I swapped flights. I was already at the airport when I called you.' He handed her a mug. 'Instant only. I'm sorry.'

'No problem.' She placed the mug on the floor and got out of the bed to pull on her jeans and jersey.

Mitch didn't even look at her. Which only went to show how bad things were. She asked, 'Is Jamie sleeping?'

'Yes. Max is sitting with him for a few minutes while I came to see you.'

She blinked. 'He sent me in here hours ago.'

'Sent Lucas home, too. Seems Max quite likes babysitting his nephew.' Mitch looked bewildered.

She changed the subject. 'How did Sydney go? Did you do everything you wanted?'

'Yes, I did.'

The coffee wasn't flash but she drank it down before her shaking hands dumped most of it over her jeans. Then, 'Mitch, I'd like to move to Sydney when all this is over so that Jamie can be near you. He needs both of us in his life—all the time.'

'Yes, he does.' Mitch stood up, paced the three steps to the door and turned, his face relaxed and open. 'I'm not going to be taking up that position. I went across to talk to the general manager of the hospital and explained the situation. I also had to cancel the lease on an apartment I'd arranged and tidy up a few things so I didn't leave a bad taste in anyone's mouth.'

'What? You're staying in New Zealand?' When he nodded, she asked, 'Where? Haven't you been replaced here?' Why was he doing this?

'The board hasn't decided on a candidate for my job; they're still doing interviews. I've been told I can stay on. So would you consider moving to Auckland rather than Sydney?'

'Of course.'

'You haven't even thought about it,' he pointed out.

'Nothing to think about. You're giving up your prestigious job. That's huge.' She would be giving up a job she enjoyed but hadn't been able to give her full attention to anyway. And then there was Mum. Who knew what Mum would do? But one thing was certain—she'd approve of this.

'It wasn't that hard. It feels right, good even. I want to get everything right with Jamie. I want to be a great dad.'

'Thank you.' Tears blurred her vision. A part of her was happy, happy for Jamie.

He returned to sit opposite her, took the mug out of her hands. Then he folded his hands around hers. Warmth seeped into her, giving her strength and courage.

'Mitch, I got it all wrong. I didn't give you a chance. I guess I hadn't learned how much you've changed, didn't want to admit you're not the man I knew three years ago. I seem to have fallen into my old habits when I'm around you and so I expect that you're doing the same. I blew it. I'm sorry.'

His fingers squeezed her tight. 'It's okay. I get that. And it doesn't matter anymore.'

Her heart dropped. So there'd be nothing developing

between them. Their up-close-and-personal encounters weren't going to be repeated. Unless she was honest. About everything.

She tugged her hands free and stood up, stepping around him while her brain worked overtime. Finally she said, 'I loved you last time. I never said so because I felt vulnerable. I understood enough about you to know you wouldn't stay for the long haul. But I loved you and when I packed your bags it nearly killed me.

'I thought I'd got over you. But I hadn't. I haven't. Coming here, seeing you again, being with you, talking, making love, even arguing, I feel complete. I still love you. I've never stopped. I—I wondered if we could try again.'

A smile broke across his mouth, his whole face, into his eyes. He reached for her and sat her on his lap. His hands cupped her face. 'Try keeping me away.' His lips brushed hers. 'You're the only woman who makes my knees knock or my heart skip. I've always loved you right from that first date when you spilled your red wine over my grey suit. You were so embarrassed because it was the only suit I owned and I had an interview the next morning.'

'Do you have to remind me?' He loved her. That had to be good, didn't it?

'You still owe me.' His smile widened into a grin. Then he grew serious. 'Jodi Hawke, I love you with all my heart. Do you think we deserve a second shot at our relationship? Will you marry me?'

Her eyes widened while inside her heart swelled with love. 'Yes,' she breathed. Leaning in, she covered his mouth with hers and repeated, 'Yes.'

He kissed her back long and hard, before pulling away. 'We've got a tough time ahead with Jamie and the transplant, but I was hoping we could get married as soon as possible. A very quiet, private service. Just you, me and Jamie. Your mum, even Max.' He stopped, sucked a breath. 'I'd feel more comfortable knowing we were legally together before I have the surgery.'

'Yes, definitely, if that's what you want.' Tears spurted from the corners of her eyes. So the surgery worried him. Yet he'd do it for his child. A true father.

There was a knock and the door flew open. 'Mitch, sorry to barge in but you're needed in the ED. Now.' The man in blue scrubs nodded at Jodi. 'Hi, I'm Aaron, Mitch's second in charge. There's been an accident on the Harbour Bridge involving three cars. We've got three priorities due within the next five minutes.'

Jodi leapt up so Mitch could stand. 'Go, Mitch. I'll be with Jamie.' She reached up and kissed him quickly. 'Yes. Absolutely yes.'

Aaron said over his shoulder as they tore along the corridor to the stairwell, 'Bad timing, huh?'

'For me, yes; for the patients, no. An extra specialist might make a difference for one of them.' Jodi loved him. Holy Toledo. They were getting married. Next week if he could get everything organised.

'So no more plans to leave us?' Aaron shoved the fire door open, shot through.

Mitch was right on his heels. 'Not in the foreseeable future.' His future involved family now. He grinned despite the urgency driving him down the stairs to his department.

The first ambulance was unloading as they reached the department. 'Yours,' Aaron told him.

'Right.' He followed the stretcher being wheeled straight into Resus.

The paramedic handed over the PRF. 'Janet Lees, twenty-four years old. Driver of one of the cars. Hit the side window with her head when the car spun. High blood loss from femoral artery.'

Nurses and interns stepped up, suctioning the patient's mouth, swapping the oxygen supply from the ambulance tank to theirs, putting in lines for fluids, applying pressure to that artery. Organised chaos reigned. Mitch oversaw everything, making decisions, ordering X-rays, working to stem the blood loss from the torn artery.

Phoning a neurologist, he said, 'Tom, I think we've got a severe brain injury due to trauma. Can you come down?'

A couple of minutes later Tom Grady blew in like a winter wind, immediately reaching for the report form and the latest obs. And Mitch continued doing everything possible to save Janet Grady's life.

But an hour later he had to step back and listen to Tom. The news was grim.

He said, 'We'll put her on life support and send her up to IC. The family will need time with her.'

Mitch sucked a breath. And swore long and hard under his breath. Tragic deaths happened. But he hated them.

The family would be asked if they wanted Janet to be an organ donor. Donation was a gift. More than one gift to more than one desperate person. But how did families make this decision at the worst possible time of their lives? He'd dealt with other cases where the patient had gone on life support until the organ retrieval team had done their thing, and he'd accepted it for what it was. Death giving life. Someone's loss giving another person a better chance at a future. Nothing wrong with that. Hell, he was signed up as a donor if something happened to him. He'd gone as far as making sure his adoptive family knew and understood his wishes. But now he suddenly found it entirely different, that the right thing to do wasn't that easy.

More than that, he finally really understood why parents might say no. Mitch took one last look at the young woman as she was wheeled out of his department and wondered which way her parents would react. Sometimes life sucked.

Handing over, he headed for the shower. He threw his filthy scrubs at the basket. Missed. Shoved the tap hard to the right. Leapt under the water. Leapt out again. 'Bloody cold.'

Thank goodness Jodi had brought Jamie to him. Thank goodness he could save his boy without anyone having paid the ultimate price.

The water was warming. He stepped into the shower again and tipped his face under the water, let it stream down his body. He needed to cleanse away the smells of the ED, then he needed Jodi's arms around him.

Jodi was curled up in a chair beside Jamie's bed when she saw Lucas walk in. 'It's two in the morning. Why aren't you at home?'

Mitch appeared behind him, looking dreadful. Not just exhausted but hollowed out. Despair oozed out of him as he met Jodi's gaze.

A trembling started deep inside her. 'No.' Her head swung from side to side. 'No.' She wasn't ready. Hadn't prepared for this enough. 'No.'

'Jodi?' Mitch lifted her into his arms and held her tight. 'It's all right, sweetheart. Everything's going to be fine.'

She'd never be ready. Jamie needed a new kidney to survive. She'd signed the papers, understood the consequences and risks, wanted it for him. But she wasn't ready for her boy to go under the knife. To have such major surgery. 'He's too little. Too frail.'

'He's tough. He's a Hawke. He's a Maitland.' Mitch spoke with conviction. With tenderness and understanding.

She shifted in his arms, looked for Lucas. 'Tell me.'

Lucas was sitting on the end of Jamie's bed, watching her. 'There's been an accident in Nelson. Two people died and one is an organ donor. The retrieval crew are on their way down there. We'll know more in a couple of hours. But, Jodi, you have to prepare yourself. It could be a match.'

Under her hands she felt Mitch's chest rising and falling far too rapidly. 'Mitch?'

His chest rose high and stuck there. Then as his lungs slowly let the air out he said, loudly and clearly, 'Lucas, phone Max and get him and his team in here. He'd be coming to do the op anyway. But he'll be taking one of my kidneys for Jamie. It's time to do it. We were only waiting for one more counselling session. I don't see the point. I'm ready.'

Lucas nodded. 'Fair enough. Your kidney is a far better option for our lad here anyway. It's a go, then. I'll go and make some calls.' He stood up and looked from Jamie to Mitch to her. 'Jodi, you're going to have the hardest job of all of us. You have to sit around waiting.'

For both my men. She wanted to shout at the world for letting this happen in the first place. She wanted to cry and fold into Mitch for his strength. She wanted to pick Jamie up out of his bed and run.

Instead she straightened her spine and looked first at Mitch and then Lucas. 'Think what I've got. Mitch and Jamie. How can I not be okay? I'll be like a soccer mum, cheering and encouraging from the sidelines.' Gulp. At

least she'd got that out without a quaver in her voice to
give her away. Her stomach turned over, wanting to reject the meal she'd eaten hours ago. No way. Not now.
She sucked her belly in against her backbone. She was
strong. And today she'd just have to be even stronger.

'I'll be back when I know more.' Lucas headed for the
door, turned back. 'Mitch, nil by mouth from now on, eh?'

Mitch nodded slowly and sank down on a chair, pulling
Jodi with him. The reality was hitting home. This time
tomorrow he'd have one kidney and Jamie would be on
the road to a full recovery. 'It's happening.'

'Faster than you'd thought.' Jodi brushed a lock of hair
behind his ear. Love radiated from her eyes. Love for him.

'Better that way. The decision's been made, nothing to
wait for. It's not as though I need to listen to that counsellor spouting on about what my emotions are going to
be doing. I get it. Time to get on with the whole damned
process.' So stop raving and give Jodi your undivided attention. Support her.

Under his hands he could feel the occasional tremor
rock through her body. But she sat straight, not melding
into him. There was confidence in her face, that earlier fear long gone. Amazingly brave. Because she really
would go through hell when he and Jamie were wheeled
away to Theatre.

Mitch wrapped his arms around her and dropped his
chin on the top of her head, smelt the lavender of her
shampoo, remembered the night he'd woken up to find
her in his office. She'd brought him so much. She'd given
him a life worth living. How did he thank her for that? A
lifetime together, cherishing her, would not be enough.

'One step at a time, boyo.'

'What are you talking about?' Jodi mumbled against
his neck.

'Thinking that our wedding will have to wait a few days.'

She sat so she could meet his gaze full on. 'We could try to get a special licence, if that's what you want.'

He shook his head. 'I think we've got enough to deal with.'

'Mitch, we're a family now. A piece of paper isn't going to change that.' She kissed her finger tip, placed it on his lips. 'I love you. More than you can imagine.'

He kissed her finger and tapped it on her lips. 'And I love you. We've got each other, and our son. We're as married as anyone who has said their vows.'

His mouth covered hers to give her a kiss full of love. A kiss that would get them through what lay ahead. A kiss that sealed them together. For ever.

Max stood in the doorway, watching Mitch holding Jodi, understanding, in his role of transplant surgeon, what they were all about to go through. The time had come.

His heart swelled—for Jamie, Jodi and Mitch.

And for himself.

How he'd manage it he didn't know, but he swore that once Jamie was out of danger, he would talk to Mitch.

Really talk to him. About the lives they'd both lived after they'd been separated. And hopefully one day in the not-too-distant future, he might be able to meet Mitch at The Shed for a friendly drink.

* * * * *

Mills & Boon® Hardback
July 2013

ROMANCE

His Most Exquisite Conquest	Emma Darcy
One Night Heir	Lucy Monroe
His Brand of Passion	Kate Hewitt
The Return of Her Past	Lindsay Armstrong
The Couple who Fooled the World	Maisey Yates
Proof of Their Sin	Dani Collins
In Petrakis's Power	Maggie Cox
A Shadow of Guilt	Abby Green
Once is Never Enough	Mira Lyn Kelly
The Unexpected Wedding Guest	Aimee Carson
A Cowboy To Come Home To	Donna Alward
How to Melt a Frozen Heart	Cara Colter
The Cattleman's Ready-Made Family	Michelle Douglas
Rancher to the Rescue	Jennifer Faye
What the Paparazzi Didn't See	Nicola Marsh
My Boyfriend and Other Enemies	Nikki Logan
The Gift of a Child	Sue MacKay
How to Resist a Heartbreaker	Louisa George

MEDICAL

Dr Dark and Far-Too Delicious	Carol Marinelli
Secrets of a Career Girl	Carol Marinelli
A Date with the Ice Princess	Kate Hardy
The Rebel Who Loved Her	Jennifer Taylor

0613 GEN STD HB

ROMANCE

Playing the Dutiful Wife	Carol Marinelli
The Fallen Greek Bride	Jane Porter
A Scandal, a Secret, a Baby	Sharon Kendrick
The Notorious Gabriel Diaz	Cathy Williams
A Reputation For Revenge	Jennie Lucas
Captive in the Spotlight	Annie West
Taming the Last Acosta	Susan Stephens
Guardian to the Heiress	Margaret Way
Little Cowgirl on His Doorstep	Donna Alward
Mission: Soldier to Daddy	Soraya Lane
Winning Back His Wife	Melissa McClone

HISTORICAL

The Accidental Prince	Michelle Willingham
The Rake to Ruin Her	Julia Justiss
The Outrageous Belle Marchmain	Lucy Ashford
Taken by the Border Rebel	Blythe Gifford
Unmasking Miss Lacey	Isabelle Goddard

MEDICAL

The Surgeon's Doorstep Baby	Marion Lennox
Dare She Dream of Forever?	Lucy Clark
Craving Her Soldier's Touch	Wendy S. Marcus
Secrets of a Shy Socialite	Wendy S. Marcus
Breaking the Playboy's Rules	Emily Forbes
Hot-Shot Doc Comes to Town	Susan Carlisle

Mills & Boon® Hardback
August 2013

ROMANCE

The Billionaire's Trophy	Lynne Graham
Prince of Secrets	Lucy Monroe
A Royal Without Rules	Caitlin Crews
A Deal with Di Capua	Cathy Williams
Imprisoned by a Vow	Annie West
Duty At What Cost?	Michelle Conder
The Rings that Bind	Michelle Smart
An Inheritance of Shame	Kate Hewitt
Faking It to Making It	Ally Blake
Girl Least Likely to Marry	Amy Andrews
The Cowboy She Couldn't Forget	Patricia Thayer
A Marriage Made in Italy	Rebecca Winters
Miracle in Bellaroo Creek	Barbara Hannay
The Courage To Say Yes	Barbara Wallace
All Bets Are On	Charlotte Phillips
Last-Minute Bridesmaid	Nina Harrington
Daring to Date Dr Celebrity	Emily Forbes
Resisting the New Doc In Town	Lucy Clark

MEDICAL

Miracle on Kaimotu Island	Marion Lennox
Always the Hero	Alison Roberts
The Maverick Doctor and Miss Prim	Scarlet Wilson
About That Night...	Scarlet Wilson

Mills & Boon® Large Print
August 2013

ROMANCE

Master of her Virtue	Miranda Lee
The Cost of her Innocence	Jacqueline Baird
A Taste of the Forbidden	Carole Mortimer
Count Valieri's Prisoner	Sara Craven
The Merciless Travis Wilde	Sandra Marton
A Game with One Winner	Lynn Raye Harris
Heir to a Desert Legacy	Maisey Yates
Sparks Fly with the Billionaire	Marion Lennox
A Daddy for Her Sons	Raye Morgan
Along Came Twins...	Rebecca Winters
An Accidental Family	Ami Weaver

HISTORICAL

The Dissolute Duke	Sophia James
His Unusual Governess	Anne Herries
An Ideal Husband?	Michelle Styles
At the Highlander's Mercy	Terri Brisbin
The Rake to Redeem Her	Julia Justiss

MEDICAL

The Brooding Doc's Redemption	Kate Hardy
An Inescapable Temptation	Scarlet Wilson
Revealing The Real Dr Robinson	Dianne Drake
The Rebel and Miss Jones	Annie Claydon
The Son that Changed his Life	Jennifer Taylor
Swallowbrook's Wedding of the Year	Abigail Gordon